THE PRINCESS
OF FAIRWOOD HIGH

Homeroom

Strange Times at Fairwood High
The Princess of Fairwood High
Triple Trouble at Fairwood High

Homeroom #2

THE PRINCESS OF FAIRWOOD HIGH

Nancy Norton

SCHOLASTIC INC.
New York Toronto London Auckland Sydney

ISBN 0-590-41930-7

Copyright © 1988 by Carol Ellis. All rights reserved. Published by Scholastic Inc. HOMEROOM is a trademark of Scholastic Inc. POINT is a registered trademark of Scholastic Inc.

12 11 10 9 8 7 6 5 4 3   8 9/8 0 1 2 3/9

Printed in the U.S.A.   01

First Scholastic printing, October 1988

Chapter 1

It was five minutes past eight in the morning when Princess Tamara left her bodyguard, Adolfo, standing out in the hallway, and entered her homeroom at Fairwood High School. Tamara was tall and beautiful, with silky dark hair, ivory skin, and eyelashes that didn't stop. She carried herself royally, like the princess she was. As usual, she was slightly surprised when everyone in the room didn't rise obediently and wish her good morning.

But of course no one has risen to bow or curtsy, she told herself. These are not your subjects, after all, they are your schoolmates. And this is not Capria, your small mountain kingdom, where everyone knows you're a princess and behaves properly. This is room 434 in Fairwood High School, Fairwood, California, where almost no one knows your true identity.

Which is as you wished. If everyone knew you were a princess, second in line to the throne, you would never fit in here.

Much as she wanted to fit in, Tamara still had a ways to go. As she passed the desks of the Connor twins, Cathy and Casey, one of them (she still couldn't tell them apart) called out, "Hi, Tammy. Nice necklace. You got it at . . ."

" . . . the Bargain Barn, right?" the other one finished. The sisters not only looked alike, they thought alike.

"Bargain Barn?" Tamara asked, fingering the ruby-and-pearl necklace which had been in Capria's royal family for generations. "I do not know that establishment."

"No kidding?" The twin looked surprised. "Cathy and I were in there Saturday and we saw a necklace just like that, right, Cath?"

Cath nodded, her short dark hair bobbing a little. "Right. You ought to go there, Tammy, it's got great junk jewelry."

Not quite sure which was worse, the insult to the royal jewels or being called Tammy, Tamara nodded as politely as she could, and moved off in the direction of her desk. The twins, short and sturdy as tree stumps, snickered for a moment at her weird way of talking. It was almost as weird as the fact that she'd never heard of the Bargain Barn. Then Casey poked Cathy and pointed toward the door. Judd Peterson had just entered the room.

Judd was lean and wiry, with spiky brown hair and a slightly mischievous smile. Casey had had him in her romantic sights ever since she'd set eyes on him the first day of school. Unfortunately, no matter how much makeup she wore or how many tricks she and Cathy tried, Judd's romantic sights were set on someone else — Piper Davids, who had also just come in.

"Never mind," Cathy whispered, as they both watched Piper smile at Judd. "We'll figure something out. We . . ."

" . . . always do," Casey said, smirking at the thought of getting Judd away from Piper.

Like the twins, Tamara was watching the mutual attraction between Judd and Piper. And like Casey, she was envious. But not because she wanted Judd. Even if she did, she wouldn't do anything about it. Piper was her friend, the first friend she'd made at Fairwood, and the only one who knew who Tamara really was. But to have a boyfriend, Tamara thought, that would truly be a way to fit in. To walk down the hall with a boy's hand on her shoulder, to meet him after school at some pleasant sidewalk cafe, to laugh with him the way Piper was laughing with Judd — it was exactly what Tamara thought a typical high school life should be.

Yes, a relationship with a boy would be perfect, but what boy? Glancing around room 434, Tamara discreetly eyed several boys, among them Eddie Baker. Complete with a ducktail, a single earring, and a leather jacket, Eddie was slouched at his desk reading a paperback. Tamara had tried to be friendly with him, but it was hopeless. Eddie didn't like her. He was always setting her down with insults, like a total boor.

Near Eddie sat T. Craig Yarmouth. What did Piper call him? Ah, yes, Mr. Junior Corporate. Button-down shirts and red suspenders — every day. Too young to be President of the United States, T. Craig had to settle for school politics, and he was constantly on the campaign trail. Extremely pushy, Tamara thought, not nearly reserved enough.

With a slight sigh, Tamara shook her head. This was not the way one fell in love. Especially not in a homeroom like 434. At the beginning of school, a computer error had left twenty students homeroomless. As a last resort, they'd been sent to 434. If it hadn't been for the computer, they probably would never have met.

That is the problem, of course, Tamara

thought. You are mismatched. You will never find love in room 434.

"Tamara," Piper's voice broke into her thoughts. "You look totally out of it. Is something wrong?"

"Ah, no," Tamara said, smiling wistfully at her pretty blonde friend. "I was merely thread-gathering."

Piper's green eyes crinkled in confusion. "Huh?"

"I was imagining how nice it would be if I were — how do you put it? — a totally American girl," Tamara explained. "Like you, Piper. With a boyfriend to step out with."

Piper tried hard not to laugh at Tamara's expression. "Wool-gathering, Tamara." Then she said, "But I only step out with Judd in secret, remember? You know how my parents feel about him. Even though that scooter accident wasn't his fault, they talk about him like he's a terror on wheels. And climbing the water tower didn't help his reputation with them, either."

"I know. But forbidden love!" Tamara sighed. "So American!"

"I don't know how American it is," Piper said. "I just know it's got my stomach tied up in knots. Anyway," she went on, "about you . . ."

5

"Yes?"

"I really think it's about time you let the cat out of the bag."

"But I have no cat," Tamara said seriously. "And if I did, I wouldn't keep it in a bag."

"It's an expression," Piper explained with a laugh. "It means to tell a secret. In your case, it means letting everyone else around here know who you really are."

Tamara shook her head. "Then no one would accept me."

"How do you know?" Piper asked. "At least if you were honest about yourself, it would explain a lot of things. Like the way you talk, and dress, and . . . and Adolfo." She laughed. "Face it," she whispered, "nobody believes that Adolfo's your brother. Those dark glasses, that three-piece suit. He looks like what he is — a bodyguard. But since nobody knows you're a — you-know-what — nobody can figure out why he's always tagging along behind you."

Tamara was about to argue when a whistle shrieked. Turning, she saw Ted Talbot, 434's homeroom teacher, standing in the doorway. Tall and blond, Coach Talbot was her idea of the perfect American boy. Unfortunately, as Piper kept pointing out, he wasn't a boy; he was a man. He was also engaged to be married.

Coach Talbot wasn't meant to be a homeroom teacher, either. He was much more comfortable coaching the football and basketball teams. But he and room 434 were stuck with each other, and Tamara, for one, didn't mind at all.

"Okay, everybody, listen up," Coach Talbot said, waving a sheaf of papers as he walked to the front of the room. "I've got a lot of announcements here." He grinned shyly. "The most important, naturally, is Homecoming. Go, Falcons!"

"What is this 'Homecoming'?" Tamara whispered. "And where is the aviary? I didn't know falconry was offered here."

Piper giggled as the coach started reading announcements. "The Falcons are the football team, remember? Coach Talbot's pride and joy. And Homecoming's the last football game of the season," she whispered back. "If the Falcons win, they'll be the champions."

Having finished reading about meetings of the computer club and tryouts for the next play, Coach Talbot got down to what really interested him. "I guess I don't have to tell you that the Falcons need everybody's support," he said. "The Bulldogs'll be tough to beat, so let's get behind our team and show 'em we care, okay? That's it — you can relax until the bell."

"Coach Talbot?" Tiffany Taylor said, "I think you forgot to mention the elections." Sleek and poised in a navy blue skirt and blazer, she smiled at the coach as if she were the teacher and he a not-so-bright student. "The elections for Homecoming Queen, remember?"

Coach Talbot began shuffling through the papers, looking for the announcement.

"Don't bother," Tiffany told him. She stood by her desk and addressed the class. "Any girl can be nominated," she said. "Then there's a schoolwide vote, and the five who get the most votes are the finalists. Another vote decides which one's the queen. The other four are princesses."

"You left out the nominating committee," T. Craig reminded her. "Sure, anybody's eligible to be queen, but it's the committee that makes up the first list."

"And I suppose you're chairperson," someone said sarcastically.

T. Craig hooked his thumbs under his suspenders. "Not yet," he said, smiling confidently.

"Not ever," Tiffany told him. She and T. Craig were in constant competition for any school office available.

"Uh-oh, a political showdown," Judd said with a grin. "Please, it's too early in the morning."

Tiffany ignored him. "There is no nominating committee this year," she announced triumphantly. "Instead, every homeroom will nominate one girl. That way, it's completely up to the students. Isn't that great?"

Everybody agreed that it was great. It was even greater that there were only five minutes left until the bell, and everyone started gathering their books and papers together.

"Wait, I'm not finished yet!" Tiffany called out. "I think 434 ought to nominate somebody. How's that for an idea?"

That got everyone's attention. Homeroom 434 was a computer error; nobody really belonged there. The latest joke in the halls was that 434 was the Breakfast Club of Fairwood High. The homeroom for misfits, rejected even by the floppy disks. Which wasn't true, of course. But now that the kids in 434 had gotten to know each other, and even to like each other a little, they were starting to enjoy their reputation.

"Fantastic!" said Judd, who got a big kick out of being labeled a misfit. "Somebody from 434 getting elected Homecoming Queen? It's like a rags-to-riches story."

Excited by the idea, most of the class forgot about watching the clock and started discussing just who from 434 might have a chance. Since they were all tenth-graders, lowest on the high school totem pole, it wouldn't be easy. But 434 did have its share of bright, good-looking girls.

"What about Piper?" Judd called out, grinning at her from across the room. "She's got this great, girl-next-door look, right? What's it called? The fresh-scrubbed look."

"Big deal," Cathy whispered to Casey. "What's so great about washing your face?"

While Piper's fresh-scrubbed face got redder and redder, the class argued about whether or not she was the right one for 434's nomination.

"She's okay," someone said, as if Piper wasn't even in the room. "But I think we need a little more flash."

"Then how about Karen?" someone else called out. "She's flashy. She wants to be an actress, right, Karen?"

Karen Murchinson tossed her frizzy blonde hair and gazed at the ceiling. "*That* is my life's dream, yes," she said in her low, husky voice. Rising from her chair, she pantomimed being crowned queen and threw kisses at the class. "How's that?"

Everyone clapped, but not everyone was convinced that Karen was the right choice, either. Other names were thrown out, including Tiffany's, and they argued back and forth for a few more minutes. Finally Tiffany held up her hand. She would have loved to be nominated, but she knew she'd probably never get elected. And she wanted someone from 434 to get it, because if they did, and Tiffany was the one who made it happen, then she'd be up one more rung on Fairwood High's political ladder.

"We've got to be realistic," she said. "The only girl in this room who has a good chance of being queen is Tamara. Face it, she's gorgeous. Not only that, she even acts like royalty, you know?"

"Yeah," Cathy called out, "like she expects people to wait on her all the time. And the way she talks, too. Like she writes everything down before she says it."

Tamara had been having enough trouble just trying to understand what Homecoming was all about. Now she started to ask a question, but T. Craig cut her off.

"I agree with my colleague," he said, rising to stand next to Tiffany.

"Your colleague?" Tiffany frowned at him. "When did we become colleagues? This whole thing was *my* idea, T.; don't try to grab any of the power."

T. Craig ignored her. "Tiffany is absolutely right," he said to the class. "Tamara would make the perfect Homecoming Queen, and I, for one, intend to do everything I can to see that she wears the crown."

Hoots and laughter greeted this speech, but no one argued with him. Tamara was the perfect choice; they all knew it.

"Well, Tamara?" Tiffany asked. "What do you say?"

"It is impossible," Tamara said, still confused. "You see, I am not yet a queen. I am only the Crown Princess."

Everyone laughed again, except for Piper, who tried to get Tamara's attention so she could explain things to her. Before she had the chance, though, Adolfo rushed into the room.

Nervous but determined, he hurried to Tamara's desk. "Your Highness, forgive me, but it's my duty to warn you to be careful!"

"Your *Highness*?" Tiffany lost her cool for a moment and looked totally stunned. "Did he call her 'Your Highness'?"

"That's what he called her, all right," Judd said. "And he wasn't joking, either."

Before anyone else could say a word, Tamara was on her feet. Her violet eyes were flashing and her voice was icy. "Fool! Buffoon!" she said to Adolfo. "Look what you have done. Barging in here without being summoned — it is *you* who must be careful!"

"But Your High — " Adolfo stammered.

"Enough," Tamara said frostily. "You are dismissed. I will deal with you later."

Adolfo bowed from the waist, then slunk out of the room as quickly as he could. Everyone else was still staring at Tamara, as if they couldn't quite believe what had just happened.

Tamara was already wishing she could turn the clock back, but it was too late. She took a deep breath and glanced at Piper.

Piper was smiling. "Well," she said, "I guess the cat's out of the bag *now!*"

Chapter 2

There were a few seconds of stunned silence. Everyone, including Coach Talbot, was staring at Tamara as if she were from another world. Which she was. Then Tiffany, who never lost her voice for long, spoke up. "Let me get this straight," she said to Tamara. "This is no joke? You really are a princess?"

Tamara nodded.

"Now *that* was a royal nod if I ever saw one," Judd quipped.

"So what are you doing *here*, at Fairwood High?" Karen asked.

Eddie lifted his head from the paperback book. "Slumming," he said.

"That's not true!" Piper argued.

"Piper is right," Tamara said, not bothering to look at Eddie. Then she went on to tell who she was, how living in the United States for a year was a dream come true for her, and why she'd wanted to keep it a secret. "Adolfo is here to protect me," she explained. "Unfortunately he carries his duties too far. He must have overheard what you were saying about wanting me to become queen, and he thought it would be dangerous for me to be so much in the public eye."

"What are you going to do?" asked Cathy.

"Chop his head off?" asked Casey.

"Don't be hilarious," Tamara said.

"You mean ridiculous," Piper told her.

"Exactly," Tamara said.

"Well, I think this is incredibly fantastic," Tiffany said. "I mean, not only does 434 have the perfect candidate for Queen, but she's already a real princess. What other homeroom can say that?"

Without missing a beat, T. Craig pounced on the idea. "What we need now is a slogan," he announced. "Something like 'For a Royal Homecoming, Make a Princess Your Queen.' "

With that, the bell rang, and everyone streamed into the hall, more excited than ever that one of 434's own might get elected Homecoming Queen. Tamara swept out of the room, followed by a cringing and apologetic Adolfo, and Judd laughed.

"Looks like he's in for a royal chewing out," he commented to Piper.

"Imagine bringing a bodyguard to school every day," Cathy said with a sneer. She and Casey kept walking with Judd and Piper, even though it was obvious that the two of them didn't want their company. "What does she think Fairwood is, anyway, enemy territory?"

"It all makes sense now," Casey said. With a slight push from Cathy, she edged her way between Judd and Piper. "That snobby way she acts and talks. I don't see how she'll ever get to be Queen, do you, Judd?"

"She's not a snob," Piper said. "It's just the way she's been brought up."

"Casey has a point, though," Judd said. This made Casey sneak a smirk at her twin. "Tamara's so different from everybody else, she really stands out."

"Yeah, like a pimple," Cathy remarked.

Casey giggled. Maybe this was a way to come between Judd and Piper — get them into a fight about Tamara. She couldn't wait to tell Cathy, so they could put the plan into action. In the meantime, here she was, walking down the hall, right next to Judd. Things were looking up.

When the twins finally had to turn the corner to get to their next class, Piper breathed a sigh of relief. It was bad enough that "Double Trouble" were in her homeroom; having them horn in on her walk with Judd was enough to make her gag.

"Earth to Piper; come in, Piper."

Piper looked up to see Judd grinning at her. She'd been so busy fuming about the twins, she'd wasted the rest of the walk with him.

"Sorry," she said. "I was thinking."

"Bad habit," he teased. "Anyway, here you are, Mademoiselle Dahveeds. French class, *non*?"

"*Oui, merci*," Piper laughed. She wished they had every class together, not just homeroom.

"Gotta hurry," Judd said, dropping the French accent and running his fingers through his spiky hair. "History awaits." Spinning around, he started to head off down the hall. Ten feet from Piper he stopped and spun around again. "Don't forget your three o'clock appointment!" he called out.

"What appointment?" Piper called back, as about twenty kids rushed between them.

"The one with me," he shouted. "For pizza, okay?"

Piper couldn't see him anymore. She stood on tiptoe and caught a glimpse of him being swallowed up in the crowd. "Okay!" she hollered.

Another secret date. If *that* cat ever got out

of the bag, her parents would take one look and call it a tiger.

By the time Piper's three o'clock appointment came around, all of Fairwood High knew about Princess Tamara. It was the main topic of conversation in the halls. And a lot of kids were saying the same thing the twins did — that Tamara was a snob.

Whenever somebody said that to Piper, she defended Tamara. What did they expect, anyway? A crown princess from Capria was hardly going to act like a typical Fairwood High tenth-grader. So what if she didn't giggle a lot, or wear high-tops, or practically faint every time a senior boy looked at her? That didn't mean she was a snob.

When school was out, and Piper joined Judd at the pizza hangout, she stopped worrying about Tamara for the moment. She was nervous. What if someone told her parents they'd seen her here with Judd? It didn't seem very likely, but still, it could happen. And if it did, she'd be grounded until she was too old to remember why.

"You mean you don't like living dangerously?" Judd joked, when she told him why she was nervous.

Piper shook her head. "I love being with you," she said. "I don't want that to stop. But

I don't like sneaking around. It was kind of exciting at first, but now it's just scary."

Judd put down his pizza and reached for her hand. "Then don't sneak anymore," he said. "Just tell your parents the truth — that you're dating Dangerous Judd Peterson."

Piper stared at him. "Do you want me to live the rest of my life on bread and water?"

"A prisoner in your own home?" Judd's eyes twinkled. "That would be terrible. But don't worry, I wouldn't abandon you. I'd even climb the tree outside your window at night and slip taco chips to you."

Piper couldn't help laughing. "There isn't a tree outside my window," she said. "How about the drainpipe?"

"Not nearly as romantic," Judd said. "But, hey, anything for a damsel in distress." Letting go of her hand, he took up his pizza slice again. "Seriously, though, I think you should just tell them. Once everything's out in the open, you won't have to be nervous."

Right, Piper thought. How could she be nervous if there weren't any more dates with Judd to be nervous about? No, she couldn't tell her parents. Sneaking around was bad, but losing Judd would be worse.

"We've got problems," Tiffany announced the next morning in homeroom. "No offense,

Tamara, but the problem is you."

"I?"

"You see? Anybody else would have said 'me,'" Tiffany told her. "That's not the whole problem, but it's part of it."

"I do not understand." Tamara looked confused. She also looked regal. She was wearing a cashmere sweater that matched her eyes and a bracelet of green stones. Yesterday, people might have thought the stones were glass. Today, everybody knew they were emeralds.

"I think I know what Tiffany's getting at," T. Craig said. "As one who has his finger on the pulse of the Fairwood High student body, I have to tell you, Your Highness, that you have a slight image problem."

"Slight?" Tiffany rolled her eyes. "Don't smooth it over, T. Her image problem is the size of your ego." Turning back to Tamara, she said, "To put it bluntly, people think you're a complete and total snob."

The twins shared a smile.

Eddie Baker yawned.

Tamara raised her eyebrows.

"You see?" Tiffany said again. "When you did that just now — raised your eyebrows — you looked like you think you're better than anybody else."

"But she doesn't think that," Piper said. It

was at least the hundredth time she'd said it. "That's just her way."

"I might know that and you might know that," Tiffany said, "but there are about a thousand kids outside this room who don't know that."

"Forgive me," Tamara said. "But I'm afraid I still do not understand why this is a problem. As Piper said, it is my way. I mean no harm."

Tiffany sighed. "It wouldn't be a problem, except for one thing. We already nominated you for Homecoming Queen."

"Ah, yes." Tamara smiled radiantly at the whole class. "I must thank all of you for that. Now that I understand it, it is an honor I am proud to accept."

Both Tiffany and T. Craig were momentarily speechless.

"Now," Tamara went on. "What is this problem of image?"

Eddie, who'd been watching the proceedings with a drowsy smile, spoke up. "The problem is, you walk like you've got a ramrod up your back, you talk like you've got marbles in your mouth, and you act like you expect people to drop to their knees every time you pass by. You don't stand a snowball's chance in a hothouse of being Homecoming Queen, because you're A-1, prime-grade unreal."

It was the longest speech anyone had ever heard Eddie make. For a moment, everybody just stared at him. Then Karen broke the silence with a dramatic groan. "Eddie's *right*," she sighed. "Alas. Tamara just isn't *normal* enough to be Homecoming Queen."

Tamara hadn't quite understood the part about the snowball but she understood enough to know that she was being rejected. At that moment, she didn't look unreal at all. She looked hurt.

Coach Talbot cleared his throat. "Well, now, wait a sec," he said. "Just yesterday, this whole team — I mean, class — was jumping up and down about having Tamara represent 434. And I already sent her name in as a candidate." He stood up straight and squared his jaw. "What do I have here, a bunch of quitters?"

"Way to go, Coach!" Judd called.

"Coach Talbot's right," Tiffany said. "This is a challenge, and 434 can't back away from it."

"Here, here!" Judd shouted.

"All we have to do is teach Tamara how to be a regular girl, that's all," Piper said.

"And may the best regular girl win!" Judd cried.

When everyone stopped laughing, Eddie spoke up again. "So how do you plan to do it?" he asked.

"Coaching," Tiffany said. "What Tamara

needs is somebody who can teach her how to act naturally."

Everyone looked at Karen.

"Wait a *minute*," Karen protested. "I want to be an *actress*, not a director. Besides, acting naturally isn't as *easy* as it sounds." Karen always talked like that, emphasizing every few words. She thought of it as her actress voice.

"Giving up already?" Eddie teased. By now, he'd forgiven Karen for dropping him when she thought she'd be going to Chopin High School, a school for the arts. But he still couldn't resist a few jabs. "I thought you theater people always say 'the show must go on.'"

"Eddie's right," Tiffany said. "Come on, Karen. Tamara needs someone to show her how to be a normal, Fairwood High person."

"I think Karen's jealous," Cathy said. "She probably wanted to be nominated."

Instead of getting mad, Karen laughed. "Why, Cathy, I didn't *know* you were such an *expert* on human nature. Of course I'm jealous," she said. "I think I would have made a *great* Homecoming Queen."

"I wouldn't have minded being nominated, either," Tiffany admitted. "But that doesn't matter now, right? What matters is that Tamara's our candidate and she needs all the help she can get."

"*Okay*, you've convinced me," Karen said.

"I'll *do* it. But I can't do it alone. I'll teach her the *basics*, like walking and talking. But we've all got to pitch in and show her the ropes — what to *wear*, where to hang out, *who* to hang out with, stuff like that."

"It might help if she stopped wearing all those royal jewels," Cathy said with a sneer. "I mean, how many normal high school kids walk around dripping diamonds?"

"But only yesterday you complimented my necklace," Tamara protested.

"That was yesterday," Cathy told her. "This is today. Take my advice and put your jewels back in the vault, or wherever you keep them."

"Ah, I see." Tamara smiled. "Then perhaps you will become my jewelry advisor. What was the name of that establishment you spoke of — The Garbage Barn?"

"Nice put-down," Karen observed, even though Tamara hadn't meant it that way. "I think you've got possibilities after all."

Chapter 3

Once she'd made up her mind to coach Tamara, Karen didn't waste any time. The two of them met outside the cafeteria at noon, and Karen proceeded to show Tamara how a normal, everyday girl got her lunch.

"First," she said, as they were waiting in line, "you *don't* stand here looking calm and above-it-all. You're *hungry*, right?"

"To be sure," Tamara said.

Karen rolled her eyes. "Just say 'right,' " she said. "When somebody asks you a question ending in 'right,' you say 'right' back."

"What if I do not agree?"

"Then you say 'wrong.' It's *simple*, right?"

Tamara smiled. "Right."

Karen grinned. "Okay, back to how to act in line. Since you're *hungry*, you want to check the *front* of the line every once in a while, to see how fast it's moving."

Obediently Tamara craned her neck to see over the kids ahead of them.

"But you *don't* do it for long," Karen went on, "because you're *too* busy talking."

"Talking?"

"Right." Karen pointed. "Watch those girls in front of us."

Tamara looked. There were three girls, and just as Karen had said, they all checked the front of the line from time to time. But mostly they talked. And laughed. And watched for boys out of the corners of their eyes.

"I think I understand," Tamara said. "Lunchtime is not just for eating. It is also a time to socialize."

"*Exactly.*" Karen looked pleased, as if Tamara had just passed a test. "You hang out with a couple of friends and find out what's going on, talk about *clothes*, check out the *boys*, things like that."

"But whom should I hang in with?" Tamara asked.

"Out. 'Hang *out*,' " Karen corrected. "I don't know. I'd hang out with you, but this isn't my regular lunch period. I skipped study hall so I could be here today."

"And Piper has lunch before me," Tamara said. "So I cannot eat with her. And since she is my only friend here, I usually eat alone."

Karen didn't say anything for a moment. Tamara wasn't asking for pity; she'd just stated a simple fact — she only had one friend in school. She's got to be lonely, Karen thought. "We'll work on that," she said now. "Maybe I can switch lunch periods or *something*."

Tamara broke into a lovely smile. "You would do that?" she asked. "But that would be wonderful. I think now I have two friends, correct? I mean, right?"

Karen laughed. *"Right,"* she said, reaching for a lunch tray.

Over the next couple of days, Karen kept teaching Tamara about the "art of acting normal," as she called it. Under Karen's constant coaching, Tamara started to drop some of her regal manners. She stopped holding out her hand to be kissed whenever she met somebody, and remembered to say "hello" or "hi" instead of "how do you do?" She took Cathy's advice and put her jewels in a bank vault, and she stopped bringing her own monogrammed linen napkins to use at lunch. She couldn't get rid of Adolfo, but she ordered him to stop wearing suits, and she wouldn't let him carry her lunch tray or books anymore.

After a dramatic speech to her counselor claiming that she studied better on a full stomach, Karen was able to switch her lunch period. So Tamara now had someone to hang out with in the cafeteria. As far as Tiffany was concerned, though, Karen wasn't enough.

"She's got to be seen with lots of kids," Tiffany told Karen one morning in homeroom. "We want everybody to think she's popular."

"I have an idea," Karen said. "I'll talk to the kids from my drama club. Some of them can *walk* with her in the halls, some can *go* shopping with her, some can *eat* lunch with her." Karen was beginning to enjoy her role as director. "It'll be like an acting assignment, sort of an experiment in *théâtre verité*."

"Get real," Tiffany said. "No offense, but the drama club kids are not exactly the kind of people Tamara needs to be seen with."

"What's *wrong* with us?" Karen asked. "We *love* what we do, we put on *great* plays, we're *passionately* dedicated to our art, we — "

"You're weird," Tiffany broke in. "A little of it isn't bad, but a whole club of artistic types would weird everybody out."

"Oh, I get it," T. Craig said. "Tiff wants to get Tamara in with the 'right' crowd, like the Student Council. The ones with political power. It's a way for Tiff to get in with them herself."

"Don't call me Tiff, T.," Tiffany said. "You probably have the same idea yourself."

"Aha! Notice she doesn't deny it," T. Craig commented to the rest of the class.

"This is ridiculous," Piper said. "You two act like Tamara isn't even a real person. Sure, she needs to loosen up a little, but she can make her own friends."

"Yes, but can she do it in time to be Homecoming Queen?" Tiffany asked. "The first vote is ten days away, and if she doesn't make the list of finalists, 434 can kiss the whole thing good-bye."

Coach Talbot cleared his throat. "Speaking of Homecoming," he said, "the game — "

But the bell interrupted him, and the kids started leaving, still talking about Tamara.

As usual, Piper and Judd left together. This time, they managed to escape the twins.

"Forget them for now," Cathy said to Casey, who was hurrying after them. "We'll think of some way to break them up."

"In time for the Homecoming dance?" Casey asked. It was her dream to go to the dance with Judd.

"Sure, don't worry," Cathy said.

Just then, Tamara walked up to them. "Excuse me," she said. "But I have planned a shopping trip tomorrow and I would like to visit the store you mentioned. What was the name?"

The twins eyed each other. Then Cathy

grinned, "Oh, you mean the Bargain Barn."

"Ah, yes, that was it. Thank you. I mean, thanks." Tamara turned to go.

"Wait," Cathy said, still grinning. "The Bargain Barn's good, but there's a better place. It's in the mall and it's called . . ."

" . . . Over the Edge," Casey finished, reading her sister's mind. "They've got great stuff."

"Over the Edge," Tamara repeated. "Wonderful. I shall — will — try it." Hoisting her books a little higher, she smiled and left.

Still grinning, the twins watched her go. Over the Edge did have great stuff; they'd told the truth about that. What they hadn't bothered to mention was that it catered to the heavy metal crowd. Wearing clothes and jewelry from there wouldn't help Tamara's reputation as a regular girl one bit.

Pleased with themselves, the twins headed for their next class. They hadn't solved the Judd-Piper problem yet, but if Tamara took their advice and went to Over the Edge, then at least they'd done some damage.

Two days later, Tiffany walked into 434 with a computer printout in her hand. Coach Talbot hadn't arrived yet, so she stood behind his desk and rapped on it.

"I protest," Judd said immediately. "I like the teacher we have. He's always late and he doesn't make us listen to the announcements unless we're interested."

"You'll be interested in this," Tiffany said, waving the printout. "I've been getting some feedback on Tamara and — oh my gosh, this can't be happening!"

Everyone turned to look where Tiffany was staring. In the doorway stood Coach Talbot. He immediately blushed and looked embarrassed at all the attention.

But it wasn't the coach Tiffany was reacting to. It was the girl standing just behind him — Tamara.

The princess looked beautiful, as usual. She also looked like the lead guitarist in a band called Snake Venom.

She was wearing a gray sweatshirt with the sleeves chopped off just below the shoulders. Her pants were skintight and looked suspiciously like snakeskin. Her hair was pulled up into a straggly topknot. Wrapped around her arms and ankles were silver cobras, and silver rattlesnake rattles dangled from her ears.

"Come in here, quick!" Tiffany ordered. "Somebody shut the door!"

"I don't get it," Tamara said.

"Well, at least you got that expression right." Tiffany pushed her hair back, looking frantic. "But those clothes!" she groaned. "Did anybody see you in them?"

"I suppose so," Tamara said, confused. "But what is wrong with my clothes?" She turned to Karen. "You said I should not dress so straight. Is Over the Edge not crooked enough?"

"You mean you sent her *there*?" Tiffany asked Karen. "I can't believe it!"

"What is wrong?" Tamara asked again, suddenly looking at the twins.

"Well, snakes aren't my favorite people or anything," Karen said, "but do you have any idea how many of them sacrificed their *lives* for those pants?"

"Oh, no," Tamara said. "The girl in the shop assured me that these were fake snake."

"Okay, but Over the Edge is just a little *too* crooked," Karen told her. "And *I* didn't send her there," she said to Tiffany.

Tiffany turned back to Tamara. "Then who told you to go there?"

The twins had suddenly become extremely interested in their biology books, Tamara noticed. She was tempted to reveal them for the traitors they were, but she decided not to. If she told on them now, they would bad-mouth her so much she would never have a chance to be Homecoming Queen. And she wanted that chance. That chance to be accepted and popular and normal. So for the moment, she would let them off the rope.

"No one person sent me," she said. Two people did, she thought. "I simply heard it mentioned and I thought I would try it." She looked down at her outfit. "It seems I *did* go over the edge."

"I'll say," Tiffany agreed. "And the next time you go shopping, take somebody with you."

"I'll go," Piper volunteered, smiling at Tamara. "I want to check out dresses for Homecoming, anyway."

"*Good*," Karen said. "Hanging out at the mall was my *next* lesson."

"You mean it's different from hanging out in the cafeteria?" Tamara asked.

"*Très, très* different," Karen said. "There's a real art to it, especially when you run into boys."

"Boys — that's exactly what I want to bring up," Tiffany said, waving her computer printout.

Before she could go on, Coach Talbot coughed. Tiffany looked at him, surprised. "I'm sorry, Coach Talbot. Did you want to say something?"

"He's only our teacher," T. Craig said to her. "Why should he want to say something?"

Tiffany blushed, then glared at T. Craig for embarrassing her. But Coach Talbot laughed. "Hey, it's okay. I think the way this group has come together to back Tamara for Queen is really terrific. I just hope the Falcons show as much team spirit during the game."

Tiffany gave a triumphant smile to T. Craig.

"Just let me read these announcements here," Coach Talbot went on, "and then you can get back to calling the plays."

Quickly the coach rattled off the announcements while Tiffany stood to one side, studying her printout.

"Who said she could call the shots, anyway?" T. Craig muttered to Judd.

"Nobody," Judd whispered back. "But she's not doing a bad job, is she? Now there's a girl who really knows how to organize things. She's got my vote," he said with a grin.

Not mine, T. Craig thought. Unfortunately Judd was right. Tiffany was a real go-getter. A computer printout, for crying out loud! He'd have to do some pretty fancy footwork to catch up with her.

"Like I said," Tiffany went on. "I've been getting some feedback from kids about Tamara. It's not bad, but it's not great, either." She consulted her paper. "Forty-nine percent — snob; thirty-nine percent — nice, but a little too stiff; eight percent — don't know; four percent — couldn't care less."

Tiffany looked up. "Just keep on with what you're doing, Karen. Once Tamara loosens up some more, I'm sure these numbers will change. And," she added excitedly, "I had a brainstorm last night that I think will really help — Tamara should have a boyfriend!"

"A *romance*!" Karen said. "It's *perfect*. A little love interest *always* makes the plot more interesting."

"It doesn't have to be a real romance," Tiffany said. "But if Tamara starts dating someone, it'll make her more real, you know, more of a regular girl."

"I have to admit, it has great image-making possibilities," T. Craig said stuffily.

Tamara cleared her throat. "I would be happy to date," she said. "But I'm afraid I have no boyfriend."

"No problem," Tiffany assured her. "We'll find one for you. From right here in 434."

The rest of the class liked the idea and immediately began discussing the merits of every boy in the room. Tamara sat silently. This was not how she had imagined getting her first date. In fact, it was extremely embarrassing.

On the other hand, as Tiffany said, they weren't asking her to have a true romance. True romance could come another time. For now, to go out with someone, the way other girls did, would be such fun.

Smiling to herself, Tamara began to daydream about going to the cinema, walking in the park, dancing at Homecoming with her date. It was such a pleasant dream that she barely heard the conversation going on around her. But then a name caught her ear, and she came back to earth with a jolt, as if someone had thrown ice water in her face.

"Eddie's the perfect choice," Tiffany was saying. "He's a little rough around the edges, but he's popular, and he's a regular guy. He's just what Tamara needs."

All her dignity gone, Tamara's mouth dropped open as she looked at Eddie Baker. This crude boy with his swantail haircut and total lack of manners was to be her boyfriend? It was an insult. She would not allow it to happen.

Chapter 4

Before Tamara could think of a tactful way to say that Eddie was a boor with whom she wouldn't be captured dead, Eddie himself was on his feet.

"No way," he said flatly. Then he sat down again.

Tiffany looked shocked. "What do you mean, 'no way'?"

Eddie didn't answer. Slouching at his desk, he pulled out a battered magazine and began thumbing through it, ignoring everyone.

The magazine was about cars, Tamara noticed. But of course. Eddie Baker must dream of the day when he could get behind the wheel of an automobile and terrorize the civilized world.

So he didn't want to date her? Good. Then

they had one thing in common — mutual dislike.

Meanwhile, a frustrated Tiffany was trying to get Eddie to take his face out of his magazine and talk to her. "You're ruining our plans!" she cried. "The only other guy from 434 who's right for this is Judd. And he's already dating Piper. You can't let us down, Eddie!"

Finally Eddie looked up. "I'll vote for her," he said. "But I won't date her."

"Why not?"

"Simple," Eddie said. "She's a snob. And I don't date snobs."

Now Tamara stood up. It was impossible for her to keep quiet about such an insult. "And you," she said to Eddie. "What are you? A Caprian peasant wouldn't even date you."

Eddie grinned, not bothered at all. "See what I mean?" he said. "This is the twentieth century and she's talking about peasants. Like I said, a snob, pure and simple."

"Now, wait a minute," T. Craig said. If he could solve this, he thought, then he'd be the hero. And Tiffany would lose some of her power. "I appeal to you as two reasonable human beings," he told Eddie and Tamara. "Nobody's asking you to like each other. We're merely asking you to pretend. Think of it as a challenge. Think of it as a duty. And remember, the reputation of homeroom 434 is in your hands!"

Judd put his fingers to his lips and gave a shrill whistle. The rest of the class stamped their feet and cheered. T. Craig hooked his thumbs in his red suspenders, bowed his head, and tried to look humble.

But Tamara and Eddie weren't impressed. And when the bell rang, they weren't convinced, either.

"Eddie, *wait!*" Karen slung her bookbag over her shoulder and edged through the crowds in the hallway. Catching up to him, she took him by the sleeve and pulled him to one side.

"Listen," she said, "I *know* you don't want to date Tamara, but it isn't a *lifetime* thing, you know. It's just until Homecoming is over. Can't you give it a *try?*"

Eddie leaned against a locker and crossed his arms. "How come you're so gung ho about this?"

"It's not just *me*," Karen said. "It's *everybody* in 434. I *mean*, imagine! Homecoming Queen, from the homeroom that doesn't really exist! It's so *dramatic*, so theatrical!"

Eddie ran his hand through his dark hair. "Yeah, well, like I said. I'll vote for her. I don't care if she's Homecoming Queen. It's no skin off my nose."

"But dating her is, huh? Oh, *Eddie*." Karen closed her eyes and shook her head. "*Eddie, Eddie, Eddie.*"

"Come on, knock off the act." Eddie couldn't help grinning. "You're not onstage now. What's this 'Eddie, Eddie' stuff?"

"Okay, you asked me." Karen shook back her hair and looked him in the eye. "Voting for a snob — which she isn't — is no skin off your nose. But *dating* one is. You're worried about your reputation, aren't you, Eddie? *Tsk, tsk.*"

"What do you mean, 'tsk, tsk'?" Eddie asked. "What's wrong with worrying about my rep?"

"Oh, nothing," Karen said. "Except it makes you just as *big* a snob as you think Tamara is."

"Now wait — "

"No, it's okay, I understand," Karen broke in. "If your reputation as Mr. Macho of Fairwood High would be *ruined* by dating practically the most beautiful girl in the school — "

"That's not — "

"Or," Karen went on, "if dating somebody with good posture and *great* manners is going to hurt your image as a laid-back guy, I can see why you'd be worried."

"Hey, will you — "

"It's all *right*, Eddie. You're off the hook."

Smiling sweetly, Karen patted him on the

arm and then headed off down the hall. Laughing would have ruined her performance, so she waited until she was sure she could keep a straight face. Then she looked back.

Eddie was still leaning against the lockers, arms crossed, head cocked as if he were listening. Karen knew he was thinking about what she'd said.

Gotcha, Eddie! she thought.

"Let's take your stuff back to Over the Edge first," Piper suggested to Tamara. "Then we can have fun."

"Fun?" Tamara looked around. It was Saturday at the Fairwood Mall, and the place was overflowing with people, shopping, eating, hanging out. "I have never been here when it was so crowded. Is getting trampled supposed to be fun?"

Piper laughed. "Don't worry. This isn't a riot, it only looks like one. Anyway, hanging out at the mall is something you should know how to do."

"Ah, so I should think of this as educational?"

"Right," Piper said, laughing again as they entered Over the Edge. "And I guess I should have told you — nobody brings their bodyguard shopping with them. Of course, nobody but you has a bodyguard, but that's beside the point."

Adolfo frowned. He'd been two steps behind Tamara ever since they entered the mall, and he wasn't about to leave now. This place was chock-full of potential danger to the princess. The thought of losing her in the midst of these berserk shoppers made him break into a sweat. He had done as she asked and dressed casually, in slacks and a sports shirt. But he wasn't about to leave her.

"I tried to get him to stay home," Tamara sighed to Piper, "but he refused. Protecting me is his job, he said, and he would do his job until my family told him otherwise."

"Well, at least he's loyal," Piper admitted. "Just don't make him carry your packages, like last time. And don't make him pay for everything, either. Here, everybody does their own dirty work."

After Over the Edge, Piper took Tamara to a store called Ups and Downs. There was no one to wait on her, and she had to paw through stacks of jeans and brightly colored cotton sweaters to find her size. She managed to do it, though, and was happily joining the line to pay when Piper stopped her.

"You've got one of each!" Piper said in disbelief, pointing to the twelve sweaters Tamara had in her arms.

"Of course," Tamara said. "One in every color. It makes sense, does it not?"

"It does not." Piper grinned. "Nobody buys *everything*, Tamara. Nobody can afford to."

"Ah, but I can."

"Ah, but you don't want everyone to *know* you can," Piper explained. "There's nothing wrong with being rich, but you don't want to show off about it. And buying twelve sweaters at eighteen dollars apiece is — "

"Going over the edge, no?"

"Yes."

"I understand." Stepping out of line, Tamara sorted through the sweaters. She kept two, in pale rose and peach, and put the rest back. "It will be easier to carry two, anyway," she said, getting back in line.

Piper laughed and paid for her own sweater. It was pale green, it matched her eyes, and it just about cleaned out her savings. But she loved it. And she hoped Judd would love her in it.

After the sweaters, Piper helped Tamara find the right kind of sneakers, some sweat-shirts and sweatpants, and a couple of short, flippy skirts that went with everything.

"Now you're all set," she said, as they bought hot dogs and fries and found an empty table by the mall's fountain. "When you come to school Monday, you'll look like a regular kid."

"And Tiffany will be able to breathe again,"

Tamara laughed. "She is something else, is she not? I mean, isn't she?"

"Something else is right," Piper agreed. She chewed a french fry and thought a minute. "But you know, her idea of having you date someone wasn't so bad."

Tamara leaned across the table. "I would love to date someone," she said sincerely. "But when I dream of a boy taking me to a dance, I do not dream of a slimeball such as Eddie Baker."

Piper nearly choked on her fry. "Slimeball?" she sputtered, reaching for her Coke.

Tamara nodded. "I heard that expression in the halls yesterday," she said proudly. "It fits Eddie perfectly, doesn't it? His hair is thick with slime."

"Grease, not slime," Piper told her. "And I don't think he uses that much. But even if he did, 'slimeball' is definitely not the right word. It means somebody who's a complete scuzz."

Tamara looked confused.

"Totally hateful and disgusting," Piper translated.

"And Eddie is not?"

Piper shook her head. "I really don't know him very well, but Tiffany's right — he's pretty popular. Lots of kids like him. Guys and girls."

"Calling him a slimeball at school would be a bad move, I see," Tamara said. She took a sip of her Coke and looked at Piper. "Do you also think I should date him?"

"Well, not if he totally grosses you out," Piper said. "But you don't really know him, so maybe you could give it a try."

Tamara sighed and stirred her ice around with her straw. It wasn't that she wanted to be Homecoming Queen so badly (although that would certainly be wonderful). What she wanted most was to be accepted. Would being seen with Eddie Baker really help?

"Ah, ladies, what a pleasant surprise!" a voice said.

Tamara and Piper looked up to find Judd standing next to their table.

"I spotted Adolfo lurking over there, next to the fountain," he said, "and I knew the princess had to be somewhere nearby."

"She's not the princess today," Piper told him. "Today she's your average girl in the mall."

"Well, then I won't kiss your hand," Judd teased Tamara. "I wouldn't want to ruin your new image."

Tamara laughed. It was too bad Judd couldn't have been the one chosen to be her date. He wasn't quite normal, either, of course.

In fact, he was what her mother would call bold and brash. But he was definitely not a slimeball.

Suddenly Tamara noticed the way Piper and Judd were smiling at each other. They are truly in love, she thought. She sighed again and then stood up.

"I must have another Coke," she told them. "Being your average girl in the mall has made me feel parched as a bone."

"Dry as a bone," Piper said.

"Parched as the desert air," Judd suggested. "Or parched as a bone in the desert air. Or — "

"Never mind," Tamara said with a laugh. "I am thirsty. I will be back in a few moments."

After Tamara left, Judd sat down next to Piper, his terrific smile lighting up his face. "So," he said, peering into her shopping bag. "What'd you buy?"

"A sweater."

"Looks nice." He straightened up and grinned at her. "Why don't you wear it tonight? To the movies. With me."

Piper felt her heart do a funny little flip-flop. Would she ever get used to being his girlfriend? She hoped not.

"I'd love to," she told him. "I'll meet you in the lobby, okay?"

"Again?" Judd's smile sagged a little. "You

still haven't told your parents, huh?"

Piper shook her head. "But don't worry. I go to the movies all the time with friends. My parents won't suspect a thing."

"I'm not worried about that," Judd told her. "I just hope you don't get all paranoid, like you usually do."

"I won't," Piper said. She knew Judd thought she was being a coward, but he didn't understand. If she told her parents about him, first they'd go through the roof. Then they'd forbid her to see him anymore. She hated sneaking around, she really did. But it was either that or lose Judd. Which made the choice very easy.

Leaning over, she gave Judd a quick kiss. "No looking over my shoulder or chewing my fingernails," she told him. "I promise."

Chapter 5

When Tamara walked into homeroom on Monday morning, everyone stopped what they were doing and stared at her. Even Coach Talbot, who'd gotten to class early, broke off in the middle of a sentence about football and looked at her.

What now? Tamara wondered, glancing down at her outfit. She'd worn her new rose-colored sweater, a pair of skinny-legged jeans, and sneakers. Her only jewelry was earrings — not diamonds or pearls, but red enamel ones shaped like two small strawberries.

Such an outfit would have gotten her thrown out of the palace at home, of course. But here in Fairwood, everyone dressed like this.

What could be wrong? When she'd looked at herself in the mirror earlier, she thought she looked perfect. Had she spilled juice on her sweater? Was a piece of egg stuck in her teeth? She ran her tongue over them. Impossible to tell.

A princess would ignore such rude staring, of course. But Tamara was trying hard to leave her royal manner behind with her royal jewels, so she asked the question any regular person would ask.

"Why is everybody looking at me?"

Tiffany finally found her voice. "Tamara, if I didn't know you, I wouldn't know you."

"Translation: You look a hundred percent normal," T. Craig said.

Piper grinned at Tamara and stuck her thumb in the air. Even Tamara knew what that sign meant. With a sigh of relief, she smiled at everyone and went to her desk.

But Tamara's outfit wasn't the only surprise to hit room 434 that morning. The minute Coach Talbot finished with the announcements, Tiffany opened her mouth to say something, as usual. Not as usual, though, Eddie beat her to it.

"I've been thinking," Eddie said. "Four thirty-four takes a lot of kidding around this school, so I guess it would be kind of fun if we could stick it to 'em by getting Her Royal Highness elected Homecoming Queen." Without even glancing at Tamara, he went on, "So if dating her will help, then okay. I'll do it. I might not like it, but I'll do it."

Karen clapped her hands over her mouth to keep from laughing out loud. She'd done it. Her remark about Eddie's image had hit him where it hurt.

"A truly humble and gracious speech," Judd joked. "I'm sure Tamara is at a total loss for words."

Tamara was speechless, all right. Eddie, the lout, acted as if he were making a supreme sacrifice by agreeing to be seen in her company. And the worst part was, she'd decided over the weekend to agree to be seen with *him*!

"Well, Tamara?" Tiffany asked excitedly. "You look great with those clothes and you're learning how to talk right. But dating is what's really going to help. So what about it?"

Tamara took a deep breath. "I accept Eddie's kind and generous offer," she said through gritted teeth.

Tiffany was so relieved she nearly fell out of her chair. "You won't regret it, you two. You'll see — you're going to help put homeroom 434 on the map!"

"Not to mention Tiffany Taylor," T. Craig grumbled. Why couldn't he have been the one to mastermind this whole thing?

Tiffany ignored him. "We don't have much

time, so you probably ought to have your first date this afternoon. Pizza, maybe. Everybody goes for pizza after school, so you'll be — "

"I think I can handle it," Eddie interrupted.

"It's just until Homecoming is over," Tamara said quickly. "That is clear, isn't it?"

"Clear as a bell," Eddie said. "I was just about to say the same thing."

Tamara nodded. "And I just wanted everyone to know that I'm doing this for homeroom 434, not for pleasure."

"In fact," Eddie said, "it'll be a pleasure when it's over, right?"

Tamara closed her eyes and took another deep breath. "Right."

"Ah, romance!" Judd commented. "Isn't it great?"

Tiffany decided to keep up a positive attitude, even though it was obvious Tamara and Eddie couldn't stand each other. "Okay, you two," she said. "You're the new couple of Fairwood High, so make sure everybody knows it. Leave homeroom together, walk down the halls together, wait for each other after school, things like that. And don't forget to smile."

When the bell rang, the new "couple" followed Tiffany's orders and left 434 side by side. But they didn't look at each other, and neither one of them was smiling.

"They look good together, don't they?" Tiffany asked as she watched them leave. She was talking to Karen, but T. Craig was the one who answered.

"They look terrific," he said. "They're about the same height, they both have dark hair and big eyes. They're a perfect match."

Tiffany smiled at him, thinking he was on her side at last. "Then you think it'll work?" she asked hopefully.

"Oh, sure, it'll work," T. Craig said. Then he grinned. "Just as long as they don't kill each other before Homecoming."

Shoulder to shoulder, and in total silence, Tamara and Eddie walked down the hall. A lot of kids called out hi, mostly to Eddie, but some to Tamara. Each time, they'd smile and say hi back. Then they'd march on, the smiles gone from their faces. Tamara felt like a puppet who only came alive when the right strings were pulled. Finally she couldn't stand it any longer.

"I believe we've gone far enough together, don't you?" she asked.

Eddie shrugged. "What's your next class?"

"History, but — "

"What room?"

"Two-oh-two, but I — "

"I'm in 208," he interrupted again. "We might as well stick together. That *is* the plan, isn't it?"

Tamara gritted her teeth, nodded, and kept walking. She'd been taught rules about how to behave in public. One smiled, no matter how tired. One looked interested, no matter how bored. And if one was angry with another person, one never clobbered him over the head with one's schoolbooks.

Tamara repeated rule three to herself. Then she counted to ten. When she was sure she wasn't frowning, she snuck a glance at Eddie. He looked as if he had just counted to ten also.

I am surprised he can count so high, she thought. Then she shook her head. Sarcasm would not help the situation.

Obviously Eddie Baker could count past ten or he wouldn't be in high school. And he must have some qualities that made others like him. Because he *was* liked, she could tell by the way kids spoke to him. She sighed. Some things would remain a mystery forever. And Eddie's popularity was one of them.

Eddie caught Tamara looking at him, and before she could turn her head away, he said, "Something bothering you?"

Tamara shook her head and counted to ten again. Whatever made him popular, it certainly wasn't his manners.

Finally, to Tamara's relief, they reached room 202. But before she could slip inside, Eddie shouldered her over to the side of the hallway until her back was against the wall.

Putting one hand against the wall, right near her head, Eddie leaned forward until his face was inches from hers. It made a perfect picture, and plenty of kids noticed. But it was a good thing no one could hear what was being said, or the image of the "happy couple" would have been ruined.

"Why are we standing here?" Tamara was asking. "This is no time to loiter. I must get to class."

Eddie almost laughed at the world "loiter." This girl was a real pain. He was surprised anyone had even bothered to say hi to her. Maybe she could fool some of them, but not him. She might be able to dress like everybody else, but underneath those regular clothes, she was still Miss Superior.

"We're 'loitering' because that's what couples do," he explained. "And another thing couples do is meet after school. So. You know where Jake's Pizza is?"

Tamara nodded. Jake's was one of the most popular hangouts.

"Good," Eddie said. "I'll see you there at three."

Finally he dropped his arm from the wall and started to move away. Then he stopped and turned back. "Oh. Leave your bodyguard in the dust, why don't you?"

"In the dust?"

"Behind," Eddie sighed. "Don't bring him, okay? After all, you don't need him anymore. You've got me now."

Grinning, Eddie walked away.

Tamara raised her eyes to the ceiling. What have I done? she wondered. And how will I ever keep from breaking rule three?

At the same time that Tamara and Eddie were making their frosty way down one of the halls, Judd and Piper were strolling together down another one.

Piper was feeling great. Saturday night's date had been perfect. Judd had loved the way she looked in her new green sweater. More important, he'd kissed her three times before they said good-bye. Then she'd run into him at the library on Sunday, which she hadn't expected to do, and they'd studied together for an hour. Judd didn't seem the type to spend Sunday afternoon at the library, but then, Judd was full of surprises. Which was one of the things she loved about him.

Now it was Monday, and here they were, together again. Piper still couldn't believe how lucky she was. She'd met Judd on the first day of school, when she'd been feeling like a very small fish in the very big pond of Fairwood High. He'd asked her out that very day, and he was still asking her out. High school life was turning out to be perfect.

Well, almost perfect. There was the problem of her parents, who thought Judd was a menace to society. If they ever found out Piper was secretly dating him, life would be the opposite of perfect.

They just won't find out, Piper told herself. Then she stopped thinking about it. It was much too nice a day to worry about that.

"I've got an idea," Judd said, breaking into her thoughts.

Piper looked at him and laughed. "Your eyes are twinkling," she said. "What's your idea? Are you going to dress up as Superman and climb the water tower again?"

"I couldn't do that," he said, pretending to be serious. "The public would start to get bored, so my next feat will have to be even more spectacular."

"I guess that's the price of fame," Piper teased.

"Sad, but true," Judd agreed. Then he laughed. "Besides, I was scared out of my mind. No, my new idea is about Homecoming."

"Don't tell me." Piper grinned. "You're going to dress up as a falcon and be the mascot at the game."

"Not a bad idea," Judd said. "Actually, though, this idea involves you."

"Me?"

Judd nodded. "And me, of course." He stopped next to the water fountain and leaned against the wall. Piper stopped, too. She was still smiling, waiting to hear what crazy thing Judd was planning.

"You don't tell your parents who you're going to Homecoming with until the very last minute," Judd said. "Like about two seconds before I come to pick you up."

"You come to pick me up?" Piper felt her smile disappearing fast.

"Right. Then I ring the doorbell, your parents let me in, and I go into my act."

"Your act?"

"I charm them with my manners, I amuse them with my wit, I astound them with my intelligence." Judd laughed at the look on Piper's face. "It's not really an act, you know. I get good grades, and I have very good manners. The wit part of it might be tricky — everybody's funny bone is different — but I'll crack a couple of jokes that are surefire laughgetters."

Piper swallowed hard.

"See?" Judd asked happily. "Before they know it, they won't be able to resist me. And they'll wonder why they ever said you couldn't date such an irresistible guy like me in the first place." He leaned over and kissed her quickly.

"Then we won't have to have any more secret dates. And everything will be perfect."

Everything almost *was* perfect, Piper thought. This was one idea she wished Judd had never had.

Around the corner from the water fountain, the twins looked at each other and smiled.

"Did you hear that?" Cathy asked. "You know what this means?"

"Yeah, it means Piper and Judd have been dating secretly, so her parents won't find out."

"Don't be thick, it means more than that," Cathy told her. "It means we've finally got some real ammunition to use against them."

The twins had already figured out a way to sabotage the new Eddie-Tamara "romance." It was simple. All they had to do was spread the word that Tamara was dating Eddie just so she'd have a better shot at being Queen. It was true, anyway. It would hurt her chances, but so what? The truth always hurt.

"This is pure gold," Cathy said now. "Once Piper's parents find out about Judd, she'll have to kiss him good-bye."

"And we're going to tell them?" Casey asked.

"Yeah, but we can't just ring the doorbell and tell them face to face," Cathy said. "Then Piper would know who did it."

"How about a note?" Casey suggested. " 'Dear Mr. and Mrs. Davids. Guess who your sneaky daughter is dating? Hint: His inititals are J.P.' "

"We already used a note against Piper once," Cathy reminded her. "When she and Judd were passing them in homeroom, remember? If we did it again, Piper would suspect us for sure. We have to think of something new." She stuck a stick of gum in her mouth and chewed furiously. "But don't worry. We'll do it. And when we do, Piper will be out of Judd's life."

"Yeah," Casey said smugly. "And I'll be right there, ready to take her place."

Chapter 6

At three o'clock that afternoon, Tamara left a very unhappy Adolfo in the record store and then walked into Jake's Pizza, next door.

Jake's was crowded, as usual. Even though it was Monday, and even though everyone had homework, it seemed to be a Fairwood High tradition to stop at Jake's, even if it was just to get a Coke to go.

It would be a pleasant thing to do, Tamara thought. If only she had a different reason for doing it. Standing just inside the door, she craned her neck, looking for Eddie. She was still looking when the door crashed into her back.

"Oh, sorry," a girl said. "Oh, Tamara, hi!"

"Hi." Tamara smiled. It was Sharon, from her history class. "I'm in the way here, aren't I?"

"Oh, everybody's in the way at Jake's, it's so crowded." Sharon laughed. "I'll bet you're waiting for Eddie, aren't you?"

Tamara looked at her in surprise.

Sharon laughed again. "Well, it's no secret, is it? I mean, I saw you two in the hall today, didn't I?"

"No." Tamara cleared her throat. "I mean, no, it's no secret."

"That's great," Sharon said. "Eddie's a neat guy. You're lucky."

Tamara kept her smile in place.

"Gee, that sounded terrible," Sharon said. "Eddie's lucky, too." She giggled. "You're both lucky."

"Yes," Tamara agreed, trying to sound happy. "We're both lucky." If Eddie could hear this, she thought, he would probably make some crude remark about the difference between good luck and bad luck.

"Well, I gotta run," Sharon said. "I just stopped to get a Coke. Hey, I hope you win Homecoming Queen." She giggled again. "But if you don't, at least you've still got Eddie, right?"

Tamara managed to laugh. "Right."

As soon as Sharon was gone, Tamara looked for Eddie again. As far as she could tell, he wasn't there. But naturally Eddie Baker would be late.

"Tamara!" a voice called. "Over here!"

Tamara looked and saw Karen waving frantically to her. Glad that it wasn't Eddie — she wasn't ready to face him — Tamara waved back and made her way to Karen's booth.

"I am so happy you are here, Karen," she said, sliding into the booth. "You must help me before Eddie comes."

"You sound *desperate*."

"I am. You see. . . ." Tamara blushed. "You see, I have always dreamed of dating, but I'm afraid they were just that — dreams."

Karen's eyes opened wide. "You mean you've *never* been on a date?"

"Well, of course I have spent time with young men," Tamara said. "But it was always very formal. A ball, or a garden party, or the christening of a ship."

"You've actually *christened* a ship?" Karen was amazed. "Broken a *champagne* bottle on it and *everything*?"

"Oh, yes. It's a lovely custom, don't you think?"

"Sure, *lovely*," Karen agreed. Also totally unreal.

"Anyway," Tamara went on, "my dates were not really dates, like they are here. And they were never private. So you see, I'm not sure how to behave." She blushed again and laughed. "I need lessons in dating, Karen.

You're an actress. Will you give them to me?"

"This is *absolutely* incredible," Karen said. "You're opening up a whole new part of the theater for me — *directing*. It's so much *more* creative than I thought. I'm going to be a better actress because of this, Tamara. *Thank* you."

"You're welcome," Tamara told her. "I'm pleased that I've helped you. Now will you help me?"

"Oh, *sure*. No problem." Karen ran her hands through her hair and thought a minute. "This is going to sound corny, but it's *true*. The trick to breaking the ice on a first date is to . . . hi, Eddie!"

Eddie had come into Jake's without either girl noticing. Now he was standing at the table, frowning at Karen. Karen knew why, of course. He didn't want to be there. The only reason he was there was because of what she'd said to him the day before.

Well, he'll get over it, she thought. Once he figures out Tamara isn't the ultra snob he thinks she is. She grinned to show him his frown didn't bother her a bit, and slid out of the booth. "Well, I'll be going now," she said brightly. "I've got rehearsal in twenty minutes." Then she lowered her voice to a dramatic whisper. "Remember now, you two are doing this for the good of 434. So give it all you've got, and break a leg!"

Break a leg? Now there were two things to break, Tamara thought. The ice and a leg. She had no idea what either expression meant, but it was too late to ask. Karen was gone, and she was on her own. With Eddie Baker.

Eddie sat down and shrugged off his leather jacket. Underneath he was wearing a bright red T-shirt. "Did you order yet?" he asked.

Tamara shook her head. "I was waiting for you."

"You should have gone ahead. This isn't the swiftest place in the world." He stood up. "How do you like it?"

"Like what?"

"Your pizza," Eddie said. "Plain, sausage, mushrooms? How?"

"Ah." Tamara's appetite had suddenly disappeared. "Plain."

"Back in a second," he said, and went to the counter to order.

I should have ordered, should I? Tamara fumed to herself. I suppose Eddie thinks simple courtesy — such as waiting for one's date — is a waste of time. I should have ordered what I wanted, and not bothered to find out what he liked on his pizza. Which is probably everything, no matter how greasy or indigestible.

Soon Eddie came back with the pizza. Sure enough, half of it was plain, and the other half

had pepperoni and sausage on it, plus mushrooms and peppers. Without a word, Eddie
took a slice for himself and began to eat.

Also without a word, Tamara got up, went
to the counter, and came back with a plastic
knife and fork. Taking a slice for herself, she
cut into it.

Eddie swallowed and stared at her. "A knife
and fork for pizza? Unh-uh. Pizza's like fried
chicken or a hot dog. You eat it with your
hands."

"But why?"

"Because," Eddie said, leaning over the table, "eating it with a knife and fork looks weird.
And the whole point of this show we're putting
on is to make you *less* weird."

Tamara looked around. Not another knife
and fork in sight.

Of course, it was very improper for Eddie
to comment on the way she ate, but she decided
not to say anything about that. She had agreed
to try dating him and she would go through
with it. This once.

Tamara put down the knife and fork, picked
up her slice of pizza, and took a bite. Oil ran
down her wrist and cheese oozed onto her chin.
She reached for a napkin, which stuck in the
metal dispenser. She yanked, and the dispenser fell, hitting her cup of soda and knocking

it over. Pepsi drenched the table. Three cold ice cubes plopped into her lap, rolled off, and splintered on the floor.

You've certainly broken the ice, Tamara thought. She reached for the napkins again and her hand bumped Eddie's. Their hands met. Their eyes met. Tamara was blushing and Eddie looked annoyed. It was definitely not love at first sight.

Silently they mopped up the Pepsi. Silently they picked up their pizza and started eating again. Tamara snuck a glance at her watch. Twenty minutes had passed since Eddie arrived. Could she last for ten more? Would thirty minutes qualify for a date?

"Hey, Eddie," someone said.

Tamara looked up to see two boys standing by the table. She put down her pizza and waited to be introduced.

"I thought you'd be over at Joe Fine's this afternoon," one of the boys said to Eddie.

"I will be," Eddie said. "I called and told him I'd be a little late. He wasn't happy about it, but . . . what could I do?" He nodded his head toward Tamara.

Tamara smiled at the boys and one of them smiled back. The other one grinned. "Yeah, who cares about Joe Fine when you've got a date, huh, Eddie?"

"Right." Eddie grinned back. "Hey, guys, speaking of my date . . ."

Tamara sat up straighter. Now he would introduce her to his friends.

" . . . you two don't mind if I spend a little time with her, do you?" Eddie went on. "Alone?"

With more grins and laughter, the boys moved off. The happy couple was alone now, and Tamara waited for something to happen. But nothing did. Eddie finished his slice of pizza and reached for another one. In between bites, he kept checking the time. He never once looked Tamara in the eyes.

Finally she couldn't stand it anymore. "If you must go, please say so," she told him coolly. "I certainly don't want to keep you from your friend."

Eddie frowned. "My friend?"

"Joe Fine," Tamara said. "The one you had to put off because of me."

"Look, get off your high horse, okay?" Eddie said. "Joe Fine owns a store that I want a job in. I had an interview with him today, but I forgot and made the date with you. So I put the interview off until later."

"A job?"

"Yeah, some of us do have to work, you know."

"I didn't mean — "

"Not everybody's as royally rich as you," Eddie broke in.

"Of course I know that," Tamara said stiffly. "And not everybody is as royally rude as you."

Eddie looked genuinely surprised. "What do you mean, rude?"

"I mean you were late today and you didn't bother to apologize," Tamara told him. "If you had to go somewhere else you should have told me. I certainly would not have insisted that you keep this date."

"I would have told you if I'd seen you," Eddie said impatiently. "And I was late because I had to get on the phone and rearrange my interview."

"You could have told me that, too," Tamara said. "Instead you arrive late and then complain because I didn't order the pizza. Then two of your friends stop at the table and you don't introduce me."

"Well, maybe I was afraid you'd hold out your hand to be kissed," Eddie said sarcastically.

"I don't do that anymore!" Tamara cried.

"Keep your voice down," Eddie told her. "And stop frowning. You want everyone to think we're having a fight?"

"I am not certain that I care." Tamara spoke softly, and she smiled, but inside she was furious. "I do not think this is going to work."

"You mean you're giving up already?" Eddie was smiling, too. "I'm shocked, Your Highness."

Tamara took a deep breath. She wouldn't be the first to quit, no matter how mad Eddie Baker made her. "Very well . . ." she started to say.

"Try 'okay,'" Eddie suggested. "Regular kids don't say 'very well.' Of course, regular kids don't make speeches, either. And I can tell that's what you're about to do."

Another deep breath. "Very well," Tamara said, slowly and deliberately. "I will not give up. I will keep on with this charade, as I promised to do. And, by the way, I asked Karen to help me learn how to behave on a date." Her smile got bigger. "Perhaps you should do the same."

It was Eddie's turn to breathe deeply. "I have to get to Mr. Fine's store now," he said quietly. "We should leave here together. I'll probably put my hand on your shoulder on the way out. But don't worry. It's just for show."

Like wooden toy soldiers, their mouths carved into smiles, Tamara and Eddie marched through Jake's, and out the front door.

By herself at a booth in a far corner, Tiffany let out a sigh of relief. She hadn't even known Tamara and Eddie would be here. But once she saw them, she couldn't resist staying to watch their first "performance" together. After all, she had a big stake in this.

They'd gotten off to a shaky start. Barely talking. Checking their watches every two minutes. But then something happened. She didn't know what, since she couldn't hear them, but all of a sudden they started to look like a real couple. Very intense. Forgetting to eat. Lots of heavy breathing. Smiling at each other like they were the only two people in the place.

You know they hate each other, Tiffany told herself, and they fooled you. So they can fool anybody. The plan is going to work, she thought happily.

At a table on the other side of the room, the twins were thinking happy thoughts, too. It was almost time to put their Eddie-Tamara plan into action.

Chapter 7

"It was not at all amusing," Tamara said to Karen over the phone that night. "It was — what do you call it? — a total disaster. Why are you laughing?"

"Sorry." Karen put her hand over the receiver so Tamara wouldn't hear her laugh again. "But the idea of you two pretending to like each other and really wanting to commit murder is hilarious. It's like a scene from a play."

"A very bad play," Tamara said. "And it will turn out to have a tragic ending if you don't help me!"

Karen started to giggle and covered it by clearing her throat. "Did you really tell Eddie he needed dating lessons? I wish I could have seen his face."

Remembering the way Eddie looked, Tamara found herself giggling, too. "No you don't. It was not a pleasant sight. And if you think that was bad, you should have seen him when I spilled my soda."

"You did that, too?" Karen broke into throaty gusts of laughter. "This gets better and better. I should never have left."

"I even broke the ice!" Tamara said, and described the ice cubes falling to the floor. "But I don't think that's what you meant for me to do!"

For a minute, the two girls did nothing but laugh together over the phone. The date had been one of the worst experiences of Tamara's life. But Karen was right — when she talked about it, it became hilarious.

Finally Karen caught her breath. "I feel *terrible, honestly* I do. It's like I *threw* you to the lions when I left you alone."

"I will pardon you this time," Tamara said. "In return, you become my dating director."

"Deal," Karen said. "Meet me in 434 half an hour early tomorrow. I'll bring a guy from acting class and we'll walk you through a date. By the time we're finished, you'll be ready for *anybody*."

"Including Eddie Baker?"

Karen grinned into the phone. "*Especially* Eddie Baker."

* * *

When Tamara walked into room 434 at 7:35 the next morning, Karen was already there. But she was alone.

"Jim Monroe was going to come," Karen said, "but he called this morning and cancelled. Are you ready for this? He's got chicken pox."

"Does he know Eddie?" Tamara asked.

"I don't know. Probably. Why?"

"Perhaps Eddie will get the chicken pox, too." Tamara grinned. "Then my problem would be solved, right?"

"Wrong," Karen laughed. "Then we'd have to find somebody else for you to date and you'd be starting *all* over again. And *everybody* in school would think that you dropped Eddie or he dropped you. There'd be all *kinds* of gossip and stuff and you'd lose votes."

Tamara held up her hand. "Please. I see the picture."

"You *get* the picture," Karen said. "Anyway, since Jim couldn't make it, I'll stand in for him." She pulled two desks together, so that their tops were facing each other. "This is a table in Jake's, *or* the cafeteria, or whatever," she explained. "Come on, sit down."

Tamara sat.

"I'm the boy, you're the girl," Karen said. "This is our *first* date. We're *both* nervous. We don't know *how* to break the ice."

73

"At last," Tamara said. "The mystery of the ice will be revealed."

"Yes. It's an expression," Karen explained. "It means getting past those first *awful* minutes when *nobody* knows what to say. Once the ice is broken, then you start to talk, to get to know each other. And after *that*, it gets easy."

Tamara nodded. "I understand. At last. So how does one break this ice?"

"Like I was going to say yesterday, it's *corny*." Karen laughed. "But the *best* way is to get your date talking about somethinng he's *interested* in. People *love* to hear themselves talk, and that includes Eddie."

Tamara thought about it. It made sense. Her grandmother — the Queen Mother — was famous for putting people at ease. And how did she do it? By asking them questions until she discovered what they really loved. Then she let them talk. And when they left her presence, they felt as if they were the most fascinating people on earth.

Of course, her grandmother was truly interested in people. She wanted them to be comfortable and happy. Tamara hardly felt the same way about Eddie Baker. But she would try.

"Very well . . . I mean, okay," Tamara said. "Let's begin."

Karen was just about to say something when

Coach Talbot walked into the room. "Hey, good morning," he said, looking surprised. "I didn't expect to find anyone here this early."

Tamara smiled. "We were, ah — "

"It's okay," he said. "I was going to work on some plays for the game, but I can find another room."

He started to back out the door, but Karen jumped up, ran over to him and grabbed his arm. "Listen, Coach Talbot, I *know* the Homecoming game's important, but could you just take fifteen minutes and help us out here? If you do, I *promise* you'll have my everlasting gratitude. I'll clean the chalkboard, I'll read the announcements for you, I'll take attendance, I'll — "

"All right, all right," Coach Talbot laughed and held up his hands. "I surrender. What do you want me to do?"

Karen smiled. "Be Tamara's date," she said.

Tamara and the coach both blushed a vivid shade of pink.

"It's pretend!" Karen told them. "It's for good old homeroom 434! And it's perfect, because you both looked scared to death, just like a real first date!"

Taking charge, Karen had Coach Talbot sit down across from Tamara. She explained the situation to him and then leaned down to Tamara. "Don't worry," she whispered. "Breaking this ice is a piece of cake. Just remember the word 'football.' "

Striding to the front of the room, Karen rapped on the desk with her hand. "All right, actors," she called out. *"Begin."*

Twenty minutes later, just as Coach Talbot was about to describe the disastrous Homecoming game of two years ago, Karen called out, "All right. It's time to wind it up!"

Tamara hadn't said more than two words the entire time and wasn't sure her voice was working right. She cleared her throat. "Oh, too bad," she said, still pretending she was on a date. "I have to be getting home. But I have enjoyed myself very much."

"That sounds a little formal," Karen pointed out. "Try, 'I had a great time.' "

"I had a great time," Tamara repeated. It was true, actually. She'd learned a lot about football, which was confusing but interesting. Capria's main sport was soccer. She knew soccer very well. Now, thanks to Coach Talbot, she knew something of football. That was surely important for a Homecoming Queen candidate.

Now that Coach Talbot wasn't talking sports, his basic shyness came back. He blushed and stammered until Karen took pity on him.

"Never mind," she said. "Tamara just needed someone to practice on. You'll *never* make it to Broadway, but you did just fine. Thanks a lot."

Relieved, the coach got up and retreated to the safety of his desk.

"See?" Karen said to Tamara, as other members of the class started to trickle in. "Just a few key questions and you had him talking your ear off."

"But what about me?" Tamara asked. "He asked me nothing of myself or my interests."

"Yeah, well, like I said, he's no actor," Karen told her. "On a *real* date, the guy would try to find out what you like, too. And he'd at *least* give you a chance to talk once in a while."

"I suppose it doesn't matter," Tamara said. "After all, my dates with Eddie are not real, either. They are just for show."

"That's right," Karen agreed. "And as long as you *smile* and *laugh* and *look* fascinated, the way you did with Coach Talbot, then Fairwood High won't know the difference."

The twins came in just in time to hear Karen's last remark. They sat down and smiled slyly at each other. Of course, there was always the chance that Tamara wouldn't be a finalist, so they wouldn't do anything until the first vote was over. But if she was a finalist, then Fairwood High would know the difference between

77

a real couple and a fake one. They'd make sure of it.

When the bell rang, Eddie walked straight over to Tamara, and put his hand on her shoulder. Surprised, she jumped.

"Relax," he said as they headed out the door. "It's just a show, remember?"

Yes, just a show, Tamara reminded herself. But an important one. And she must perform well. She racked her brain, trying to think of a way to get Eddie talking. It had been easy with Coach Talbot. But she wasn't sure that Eddie had such a passion for football. Still, there was only one way to find out.

Just as she was about to ask him, Eddie turned to her. "Listen," he said. "About yesterday. You were right — I was rude. I'm sorry."

More surprised than ever, Tamara glanced at him. His dark eyes were serious. He means it, she thought. This is not just part of the act.

Tamara smiled, a beautiful, bright smile that lit up her violet eyes. Nobody passing them in the hall could help but notice. Several kids nudged each other and grinned. It looked like love.

"Very well . . . I mean, okay," Tamara said to Eddie. "Thank you."

Eddie nodded, but didn't say anything more.

It's up to you, Tamara thought. It's time to put Karen's advice to the test. "Tell me," she said cheerfully, "do you think the Falcons will be able to perform an onside kick if they have to?"

Eddie stopped and stared at her. "A what?"

"An onside kick," Tamara said. She was sure she had the term right. "It's a — "

"I know what it is." Eddie started walking again, glancing at her out of the corner of his eye. "Well . . . no, I don't think they can do it. It's a pretty tough play to pull off."

"Coach Talbot thinks they can."

Eddie laughed. "Sure he does. He's the coach. He has to believe in them."

"Are they such a bad team?" Tamara asked. We're talking, she thought. We are actually carrying on a civilized conversation.

"No, they're not bad," Eddie said. "It's just — " He broke off and stared at her again. "What is this?" he asked. "Are you really interested in football?"

"I'm learning to be," Tamara told him. "But if you are not, I will change the subject."

Eddie shook his head, obviously confused at the way she was acting. "It's okay, football's fine."

"Good," Tamara said. "Now, about the onside kick. I will tell you what Coach Talbot said, and you can decide for yourself."

During the rest of their walk, the two of them discussed football and the Falcons' chances of winning the Homecoming game. Actually Tamara did most of the talking. Eddie was too busy wondering why she'd developed this sudden interest in the game to do more than nod once in a while.

Tamara didn't mind Eddie's quietness. At least he was being polite. Still, by the time they reached her history class, she decided that football wasn't his favorite subject. If they were going to keep being seen together, then she must find something else to talk about. If she didn't, they would probably start insulting each other again.

"Well," Eddie said, outside the classroom door. "It's been . . . uh . . . interesting."

"Thank you," Tamara said. She was racking her brain for another subject.

"Listen, I'll be busy in the afternoons from now on. We'll have to see each other at night, I guess," Eddie told her. "I'll talk to you about it tomorrow morning."

"Very . . . all right." Tamara started to go into class when it suddenly hit her. "The job," she said, turning back to him. "Did you get the job?"

"Yeah, I did." Eddie looked very happy about it.

"Wonderful!" Tamara said. She was just as

happy, but for a different reason. "Now we have something to discuss the next time."

Suddenly realizing what Tamara had been doing with all the talk about football, Eddie burst out laughing. But it wasn't a sarcastic laugh. In fact, it was almost friendly.

"Right," he said. "Now we have something to talk about."

Still laughing, he walked off down the hall. Tamara was unreal.

Chapter 8

On Tuesday, Piper walked into room 434 ten minutes late. Coach Talbot had already finished reading the announcements, and Tiffany was all set to give the results of her latest "Tamara Popularity Poll."

Judd gave Piper a questioning glance, but Piper pretended to be busy with her French homework. She'd been late on purpose, just so she wouldn't have to talk to him. Now all she had to do was find a way to get to her next class before he caught up with her. Because when she told him what had happened, he'd probably laugh and say, so what? And as far as Piper was concerned, it wasn't a laughing matter.

Someone had called her house the night before. Her father had answered, and whoever it was had asked for Judd. When her father said there was no Judd Peterson living there, Piper nearly choked on her spaghetti.

Then her mother said, "Judd Peterson? Isn't that the boy we told you not to get involved with, Piper?" And Piper had to say yes.

Thank goodness, her parents didn't ask any more questions. They thought the whole thing was just a funny coincidence.

Yeah, really hilarious, Piper thought. She wasn't sure it was a coincidence, either. She knew Judd's phone number, and it wasn't anything like hers. Had somebody called and asked for him, hoping her parents would get suspicious? Somebody who knew she was seeing Judd against their wishes?

She looked around homeroom, but she didn't have to look far. The twins, of course. A trick like that was right up their alley. She stared at them. Maybe if she stared long enough, they'd feel guilty. But that was impossible. Double Trouble didn't know the meaning of the word.

If the twins did it, Piper thought, then they'd probably do it again. And even if they didn't do it, even if it had just been a coincidence, it almost didn't matter. What mattered was that she was now so nervous about seeing Judd that she'd run out of fingernails to chew.

And Judd wanted to come to her house on Homecoming night! That's all she needed. She knew she'd have to tell him no, but she wasn't ready. Not yet. Maybe if she could avoid him for a day or two, he'd forget about the idea.

Piper stared at her homework. French verbs, irregular ones, the ones that always gave her trouble. Today, though, she didn't mind. At least they weren't as irregular as her life.

While Piper was wondering how she was going to straighten out the mess she was in, Tiffany was fretting about Tamara.

"Friday is the day of the vote, and today is Tuesday," she said. "That doesn't give us much time, not if we want Tamara to be a finalist. My poll shows that more people are warming up to her, but it's still not enough. I think we need some kind of extra push. Does anyone have any ideas?"

"How about if we stuff the ballot boxes?" Judd suggested. "Just kidding!" he said, when Tiffany gave him a dirty look.

T. Craig cleared his throat. "As a matter of fact," he announced, "I had a brainstorm just last night."

Everyone automatically looked toward Judd's desk.

Judd grinned. "Okay, I can't resist it," he said. "Considering the size of your brain, T. Craig, it must have been the smallest storm on record."

Thumbs hooked in his red suspenders, T. Craig waited for the laughter to stop. "All right, you juveniles have had your fun. Are you ready to listen?"

"Go ahead, T.," said Tiffany. "What's your idea?"

"It's this — I firmly believe that Tamara's image could use even more improvement." T. Craig was in his speech-making stance — feet slightly apart, one hand chopping the air as he made his case. "Yes, she's learning to talk normally. Yes, she's being seen with a popular guy. Why he's popular, I'm not sure, but that's beside the point. . . ."

"So what *is* the point?" Tiffany asked.

"It's this." T. Craig puffed out his chest. "As you know, I'm chairman of the decorating committee for the Homecoming dance, and — "

"Hey, really?" Cathy asked. "Then you can tell us what the decorations are going to be."

"Oh, I'm afraid that's top secret," T. Craig said pompously.

"I won't tell anyone," Cathy said. "Promise."

Hah! Piper thought. Telling the twins a secret is like taking out an ad in the newspaper.

"Sorry. My lips are sealed," T. Craig said to Cathy. "Anyway, my idea is this: Tamara should join the committee and work on the decorations. Let people see her getting her hands dirty. Let people know she's just one of the gang. Let people realize she's not above hard work!"

If T. Craig expected applause for his speech, he must have been disappointed. But he did get a nod from Tiffany.

"I like it," Tiffany said. "It'll be a definite plus for her image. Good idea, T. And she'll be good at it. She worked on the decorations for the Fall Frolic, remember?"

T. Craig nodded back. A compliment from your rival was also a real plus. "Well, Tamara?" he asked. "What do you say?"

"It is fine with me," Tamara said. "I do not know much about decorating, but — "

"But she can tell you anything you want to know about an onside kick," Eddie broke in.

Tamara looked at him. His dark eyes were gleaming. Was he making fun of her?

The rest of the class was mystified. What was Eddie talking about?

"Hey, it was a joke," Eddie said. He glanced at Tamara. "Just a joke, okay?"

Tamara wasn't sure what was so funny about it, but she decided not to say so. She and Eddie might get into another argument, and she didn't want that. Turning to T. Craig, she said, "I would be happy to serve on the decorating committee."

"Great," Tiffany spoke up for T. Craig. "And I just had an idea, too. Tamara's dating Eddie and that's fine. Now how about a double date? Eddie and Tamara and Piper and Judd. What do you say?"

As the bell rang, Judd stood up and said, "I second the motion!" Then he turned to Piper's desk, expecting her to agree. But Piper was already out the door.

That afternoon, Tamara reported for work in the gym. T. Craig was there, of course, and so were about fifteen other kids. Tamara knew a few of them, and they seemed glad to see her.

"It's not going to be easy," T. Craig was saying. "For one thing, we can only use one side of the gym to work in because the wrestling team needs the rest of it. For another, if we get any paint on the floor, they'll have our necks, so be sure to use the drop cloths. And, of course, I don't have to tell you to keep anything you see here a secret. I want these decorations to be a complete surprise."

The girl standing next to Tamara laughed. "I'm surprised he doesn't make us take a blood oath or something," she whispered.

Tamara laughed, too. "He probably thought of that already and decided the entire committee would quit. Poor T. Craig. He'll just have to trust us."

The girl looked at her curiously. "Hey, aren't you the princess? The one from Corfu?"

"Capria," Tamara said. She started to tell her where Corfu was and then changed her mind. The girl didn't want a geography lesson. "Yes, I am a princess. In Capria. But not here."

"I thought so," the girl said. "I've seen you around with Eddie Baker. What are you doing here in the gym?" she asked bluntly. "I thought you'd be with Eddie."

"Ah, Eddie," Tamara said. "Well, I would be with him, naturally. But Eddie has a job now in the afternoons."

The girl frowned as if she thought Tamara didn't care about the dance at all. "So this is just a way to pass the time, huh?"

"Not exactly." Tamara decided to be honest. Or partly honest, at least. "You see, I'm hoping to be a Homecoming Princess. Possibly even the Queen. But not many people know me, so how can they vote for me?" She gestured toward the other kids in the gym. "This is a way to become known."

"Okay," the girl said. "That makes sense."

"Yes, and it will probably be fun, as well." Tamara lowered her voice. "Especially if T. Craig keeps behaving like a pompous fool. Then we will have a lot to joke about."

"That's for sure," the girl laughed.

Good, Tamara thought. I might not have a vote, but perhaps I have a friend.

Ten minutes later, Tamara was on her hands and knees, stenciling yellow leaves onto a long bolt of red paper. Red and yellow were Fairwood High's colors. T. Craig pointed out that they were also the colors of autumn. And Homecoming came at the end of autumn. Which was why he had decreed that "Autumn Leaves" was the perfect motif — as he insisted on calling it — for the dance decorations.

"It's a play on words, get it?" he asked Tamara. "Autumn *leaves*?"

Tamara brushed her hair out of her face and gave him her most royal smile. "Yes, T. Craig. I get it."

Pleased with himself, T. Craig moved on to the next group of stencilers.

Tamara and the girl she'd spoken to earlier looked at each other, their faces red from holding the giggles inside.

"Autumn *leaves*, get it?" the girl whispered out of the side of her mouth.

Tamara couldn't hold back any longer. But she really didn't want to hurt T. Craig's feelings, so she made a mad dash for the gym doors. Once she was in the hall, she burst out laughing. She'd been right — this was going to be a lot of fun.

She was still laughing when Piper came around the corner. But once she saw Piper's face, she stopped.

"What is wrong?" she asked. "You look like a nervous disaster."

"Wreck," Piper said. "And I am! I can't believe I'm doing this. It's crazy!"

"What is crazy? What are you doing?"

Piper leaned against the wall, shaking her head. "I'm hiding from Judd."

Tamara looked confused. "This is not a game of hide-and-search? You truly do not want to be found?"

"I truly do not want to be found," Piper said. "Not now, anyway. And it's seek. Hide-and-seek," Piper said automatically.

Tamara was silent.

"Don't you want to know why?" Piper asked.

"Of course," Tamara said. "But one . . . I . . . shouldn't ask. After all, it is private."

"Lesson number fifty-eight," Piper said. "Regular kids always ask why. Especially if they're friends. Besides, I have to tell somebody or I really will go crazy."

Tamara smiled. "Okay. Why?"

Quickly Piper told her about the phone call. And about Judd's plan to pick her up for the Homecoming dance and charm the socks off her parents. And about how she just couldn't go through with it, but she didn't know how to tell him. Then there was Tiffany's bright idea about the double date with Eddie and Tamara.

She wasn't sure she could handle that, either.

"So," she finished, "until I figure out what I'm going to say to him, I don't even want to see him. And that's terrible. Because I can't stand not seeing him."

Tamara didn't know what to say. She'd never been in such a situation. She was having enough trouble just learning how to dress and speak like a normal Fairwood High girl. Something told her that there weren't any lessons for this kind of thing, anyway. She'd have to — what was Karen's expression? — play it on her ear.

"I don't know what to tell you to do about Judd and your parents," she said to Piper. "But if you tell him about the phone call, I am sure he will understand why you are upset. You can't hide from him forever, you know. He is in homeroom every day."

"I don't want to hide from him forever," Piper said. "Just long enough to think of what to do."

"Then I have the solution for that." Tamara laughed and pointed toward the gym. "Come and join the decorating committee. You can think as you paint. And T. Craig will have someone else to boss around. Which will make him snap his suspenders with joy."

"Well, I don't want to miss that," Piper said,

laughing, too. "Come on, let's go put some joy into T. Craig's life."

Tamara was right, naturally. Piper couldn't hide from Judd forever. And when she saw him the next day in homeroom, he didn't even realize that she *had* been hiding. It didn't matter anyway, because she still hadn't decided what to do about Homecoming.

She did tell him about the phone call, though. And Tamara had been right again. He understood why she was nervous. But Piper had been right, too — he laughed.

"Look, maybe the twins did it and maybe they didn't," he said. "But so what? Homecoming's only ten days away. And then everything will be in the open."

Right, Piper thought. And I'll be in the doghouse.

Chapter 9

At first, Piper was the only one in homeroom who was chewing her fingernails. But by Friday, the day when Fairwood High would vote for the finalists for Homecoming Queen, almost everyone in 434 had at least one ragged nail. If Tamara made it into the final five, she'd at least be a princess. If she didn't make it, she'd still be a princess, of course. But not the kind that would make 434 famous.

"I guess I don't have to tell everyone to vote," Tiffany reminded the class.

"Or *how* to vote," T. Craig said.

"When will we know who the finalists are?" someone asked.

"Monday," Coach Talbot said. "The names will be read over the PA system first thing in the morning."

"Hey, how about a pep talk, Coach Talbot?" Judd suggested.

The coach blushed. "My pre-game speeches wouldn't work for this," he said. "But I like the way you guys have come together on this thing. You're my kind of team, win or lose."

"Very nice," Tiffany said, as everyone cheered. "And I'd just like to thank Karen and Eddie for helping."

Karen stood up and took a dramatic bow. Eddie yawned.

"Well, what about Tamara?" Piper asked. "Isn't anybody going to thank her?"

"I was just about to," Tiffany said. "Thank you, Tamara. You've tried really hard to be normal, and you've almost made it."

"Almost?" Tamara asked.

"Well, you'll never be a hundred percent like everybody else," Tiffany told her. "There's still something a little different about you, and it's not just the accent. But that's okay," she added. "In fact, it's probably good. I mean, who wants to vote for a cardboard cutout?"

"Good point," T. Craig said. "That's exactly why I wear suspenders."

"Gee," Judd said, "I thought it was to hold your pants up."

"Anyway," Tiffany went on, "don't forget to keep on doing what you've been doing, Tamara.

Especially if you're a finalist. Then it'll be more important than ever."

"I won't forget," Tamara said. "I suppose I could try to get rid of my accent."

"No, don't. My poll shows that people think it's cute," Tiffany told her. "But what about that double date? Did you four ever go on it?"

"I've been trying," Judd said, looking at Piper. "So far, nobody can get together at the same time."

Piper nibbled her thumbnail.

The twins exchanged a glance. Piper and Judd weren't seeing each other as much. The call had been a success.

"Well, keep on trying," Tiffany urged as the bell rang and everyone scrambled for the door. "Don't forget, even if Tamara's a finalist, the contest isn't over!"

Out in the hall, Judd caught up with Piper and grabbed her arm. "Well?" he asked. "What about that double date? Are we going on it or aren't we? In fact, are we ever going on any date again, double or not?"

"Sure we are," Piper said, trying to sound casual.

"Good." Judd grinned. "How about after school today? Just the two of us. We can save the double for another time, like Tiffany said."

"I can't this afternoon," Piper told him. She

hoped she didn't sound relieved. "I'm working on the decorations, remember?"

"Oh, right. Well, I wouldn't want to take you away from T. Craig. What about tomorrow?"

"Tomorrow?" Piper thought fast. "Well, Tamara and I are going shopping tomorrow. For dresses. For the Homecoming dance."

Great, Piper thought. Why did you mention the dance? Now he'll start talking about meeting your parents.

But Judd didn't mention her parents. Instead, he smiled at her. It was his same great smile, just a little lopsided. "Well, look, let me know, will you?" he said. "I'll be ready when you are."

"Okay."

"And don't worry about finding the perfect dress," he said. "You'll look great in anything." He squeezed her hand and left her standing in front of the door to her French class.

Feeling guilty and miserable, Piper watched him go. How much longer could she keep this up?

"How much longer *can* you keep it up?" Tamara asked her the next day at the mall.

"Not much," Piper admitted. "I've got to tell him that he can't pick me up for the dance. And since the dance is next Saturday, that doesn't give me much time."

Tamara nodded. "That doesn't give me much time, either."

Piper stopped searching through the rack of dresses. "For what?"

"To get a date for the dance," Tamara said. "Of course, I could go alone. I understand that a lot of kids do this."

"Well, sure. But I thought you'd be going with Eddie."

Tamara shrugged. "Eddie has not asked me."

"But he doesn't have to, does he?" Piper asked. "I mean, I just thought it was kind of all set. You know, part of the act."

"With Eddie, nothing is set," Tamara said. Then she giggled. "Except maybe his hair."

"Hey, that was good," Piper said, laughing, too. "But you don't really think he sets his hair, do you?"

"No, not really. And you were right," Tamara told her. "He doesn't oil it. I examined it very carefully when we walked down the hall together." She giggled again. "The look he gave me! As if my marbles were on the loose."

"Don't worry about it," Piper said. "He probably decided you were admiring it." She pulled a dress from the rack and held it up against her. "How's this?"

Tamara stood back and took a careful look.

The dress was a pale yellow knit that buttoned up the front, and had a short skirt and long sleeves. "Do you really trust my fashion opinion?" she asked.

"It's getting better." Piper laughed. "Besides, when it comes to looking special, I'd go to you before I went to anyone else."

"Then the style is right, but not the color," Tamara said. "It is too pale with your hair. A rusty orange would be perfect."

The only other color the dress came in was black, though, so the two girls left that shop and headed for another. Piper saw something she might like in the window of one, but the store was so crowded Tamara decided to wait outside. If Piper found something, then she would go in. After years of having a dressmaker come to her suite in the palace, Tamara still wasn't used to elbowing her way around a crowded boutique.

For a minute, Tamara peered in the window of the shop, watching. But soon Piper wandered toward the back, and Tamara lost sight of her.

Turning around, she saw a vendor selling hand-painted notecards. She bought several to send to her family, then turned to go back to Piper. Piper was still nowhere to be seen.

Tamara walked a few steps in another direction and found herself in front of Joe Fine's

Pet Shop. Suddenly she remembered that this was where Eddie worked.

They had talked about it, of course, during their daily hall walks to her history class. Or rather, she had asked questions and Eddie had answered, usually in words of two syllables or less. "Do you like the job?" "Sure." "Is it difficult?" "No." "Do you like the animals?" "Most of them."

Tamara sighed. She and Eddie had reached a kind of truce. They were very careful not to do or say anything that would lead to another argument like the one they'd had at Jake's. And she was glad of that. Still, it was getting harder and harder to pretend. She almost wished they *would* argue and insult each other again. At least it would melt the ice between them.

She started to go back to the boutique and then stopped. Since Eddie started working, they hadn't dated at all. It would be good for her image to be seen with him outside the halls of Fairwood High. Besides, she liked animals.

Confess, Tamara, she said to herself. You're curious. You cannot believe that Eddie Baker, with his black leather jacket and his big hands, really takes care of such soft, small creatures as kittens and puppies.

Having confessed to herself, Tamara pushed open the door to the pet shop and stepped inside.

Joe Fine, she discovered immediately, did not sell only kittens and puppies. Although there were plenty of those, there were also fish. Thousands of them, it seemed, of every size and color, swimming endlessly in their tanks.

There were ferrets, too. And gerbils, of course. And in a glassed-off section of the shop, closed to the public, Tamara saw tanks with spiders and snakes in them. Big spiders and even bigger snakes.

Shuddering, she left those creatures and walked around until she came to the section where the birds were kept. She had heard them the minute she walked in, but seeing them was something else. Not only parakeets, but love birds, parrots and macaws, in every color of the rainbow.

She was watching a violet-blue macaw climb to his perch when a voice behind her said, "If you're patient enough, he'll talk to you."

It was Eddie. Without the black leather. Instead, he wore a white cotton jacket, something like a doctor's. He didn't look happy to see her, Tamara thought. But he didn't look unhappy, either.

"I was shopping," she explained, "and I saw the sign so I came in." She glanced around. "You never said this was such a grand store."

"You like it?"

"Oh, very much. Except for the spiders and snakes."

Eddie smiled, and his teeth were as white as his jacket. "I'm not crazy about them, either."

Silence. Tamara looked at the bird. Its head was cocked; it seemed to be watching her. "Hello," she said softly. The bird didn't blink.

She turned back to Eddie. "I don't mean to keep you," she said. "If you have things you must do, please go ahead."

"It's all right," he told her. "I'm off in a few minutes anyway. Besides, you're the customer."

"Then I must confess — I don't plan to buy anything."

"It's all right," he said again. "Most people don't. This is more like a zoo than a store. People come in to look. Oh, we sell puppies and kittens and fish. Mr. Fine could stay in business just with that."

"Then why does he have all the rest — the snakes and exotic birds — if they don't sell?" Tamara asked.

"He says it would be boring without them." Eddie smiled again. "He won't admit it, but he loves them all. Even the snakes."

Tamara stared at him. He was relaxed, comfortable, as if he'd forgotten he was talking to a prime-grade snob. "And except for the snakes and spiders, do you love them, too?" she asked.

"Yeah, I do," he said. "I like taking care of them, getting to know them. That's why I wanted this job. I tried to get one at a vet's, but I didn't have any experience. Maybe this'll help."

"Is that what you want to be? A veterinarian?"

"Maybe." Eddie shrugged. "I haven't thought that far ahead yet."

Tamara couldn't help feeling slightly amazed. "And I thought you liked cars."

It was Eddie's turn to stare. "I do like cars. What's that got to do with it?"

"Nothing," Tamara said quickly. How could she explain that whenever she thought of him, which was as seldom as possible, she always pictured him behind the wheel of a fast, loud, flashy car?

"I get it," Eddie said. "You're trying to pick a subject to talk about, right? Like football?" He laughed. "Well, now you know. With me, it's animals."

"But I tried to talk about your job before," Tamara said. "And you were about as talkative as an oyster."

"A clam."

"Yes. You didn't seem interested."

"I didn't think *you* were. I thought it was

just part of the show we've been putting on."

"So? Even if we must put on a show, at least we can try to enjoy it!" Tamara cried. "And I *am* interested in this job of yours. I like animals, too!"

"Okay, then!" Eddie said. "Next time I walk you to history, I promise to be more talkative than an oyster."

"Good! It is a deal. We will discuss animals!" Tamara took a deep breath. "If we have to, of course."

"If we have to?" Eddie frowned. "Oh, I get it. If you aren't a finalist, then our show is over, right?"

"Right," said Tamara.

"Right," said another voice.

Tamara looked at the bird. "Right," she said again.

"Right," said the bird. "Right, right, right."

Eddie and Tamara laughed.

"Does this bird have a name?" Tamara asked.

Eddie nodded. "His name's Grapejuice."

Tamara walked closer to the cage. "Hello, Grapejuice."

The bird cocked its head and said, "Hello, Grapejuice."

"He just repeats things," Eddie whispered. "He can't really carry on a conversation."

"You are amazing," Tamara told the bird.

The bird told her the same thing.

Tamara laughed again. "He even imitated my accent. He's wonderful."

"Yeah," Eddie agreed. "He's the biggest attraction in the store."

Tamara suddenly noticed the time. "I have been here so long," she said. "I didn't even notice. And you said you were off soon. I must have kept you."

"That's okay," Eddie told her. "It's . . . I . . . it was fun."

It was true, Tamara realized. She had spent time with Eddie Baker and it had actually been fun. "Perhaps I will come back," she said.

Eddie smiled. His smile changed his face, Tamara noticed. Made it softer, not so rough-looking.

"Well," she went on quickly. She was a little flustered by that smile. "I must go. Piper will be looking for me."

She walked to the door, and just as she was about to pull it open, Grapejuice called out, "Good-bye, Princess!"

Tamara left the store laughing. The ice was cracking at last.

Chapter 10

No one was late getting to homeroom on Monday morning. The tension in the room was so high that, for once, everyone was quiet. Coach Talbot was able to read the announcements without a single interruption from anyone. Of course, nobody was listening to him, but they weren't talking to each other, either. All eyes were on the speaker on the wall, every ear was waiting for its first crackle.

I just hope it doesn't come out all garbled, Tiffany thought. She had dressed carefully, as usual, in a dark green dress with a paisley scarf at the neck and tiny gold hoops in her ears. It was important to look her best, even though Tamara was the candidate, not her. Because if Tamara was a finalist, Tiffany would get a lot of the credit. And who knows? She might even be asked to make a speech.

T. Craig was in campaign clothes, too. His white button-down shirt and maroon suspenders were topped with a sports jacket, and his shoes were shiny as mirrors. He was also sitting on the edge of his seat, and not just because he was nervous, either. If Tamara made it, he had a speech of congratulations ready. And he had to be fast on his feet, or Tiffany would beat him to it.

The two political hopefuls eyed each other and then looked away quickly.

Karen caught the look and grinned to herself. What incredible egos they had. Not that there was anything wrong with that. Her ego wasn't exactly tiny. But right now, she wasn't thinking about herself much. She really hoped Tamara was a finalist. The girl had turned out to be much nicer than Karen had expected. And she'd tried so hard to be just like everyone else, which she never would be. But Karen admired her for it. It was an honest performance. Besides, thanks to Tamara, Karen now had an authentic accent she could use onstage someday.

Piper had a case of the jitters, too, of course. But for once, it wasn't because of Judd. Not that that problem was solved, but right now, she just wanted the list of finalists to be announced. And she wanted Tamara's name to be on it. If it wasn't, then Fairwood High didn't deserve to have the word "fair" in it.

Suddenly the loudspeaker crackled. Everyone jumped. It crackled again, and then went quiet.

Karen threw back her head and groaned. "*This* is as bad as waiting for the curtain to go up."

The twins gave each other a hopeful glance. They wanted Tamara to make it. If she did, they could have so much fun with their rumor.

Everyone shifted nervously in their seats. Except Eddie. He wasn't the nervous type. But he wasn't reading a magazine, either, and he wasn't slouching.

Of all of them, only Tamara seemed calm. No matter what was happening, she'd been trained to appear gracious and relaxed on the outside. Inside, her heart was beating like crazy.

Finally the loudspeaker sputtered to life again. After a few seconds of hissing and crackling, the principal's voice could be heard.

"Good morning, students," he said. "I have a long list of announcements to read, but first, the one you've all been waiting for. The votes have been tallied, and here are your five choices as finalists for Fairwood High's Homecoming Queen."

No one in room 434 heard any of the other announcements the principal had promised to read. Tamara had made it, and the minute they heard her name, the class erupted into cheers so loud that a worried Adolfo stuck his head in to make sure Her Royal Highness wasn't in the middle of a riot.

It was a riot, all right. But a happy, friendly riot, with Tamara getting so many hugs and slaps on the back she thought she'd lose her breath. But she didn't care. Her calm, gracious expression was gone, and she returned the hugs with a smile so bright it lit up the room.

"This is fantastic!" Judd cried jubilantly. "Four thirty-four is respectable at last! Wait a minute, what am I saying?" he added. "I don't want to belong to a respectable homeroom."

"Don't worry, Judd," T. Craig assured him. "With you in it, 434 will never be entirely respectable."

T. Craig had completely forgotten the words to his congratulatory speech. Which was all right, since no one would have heard him anyway.

"This is just the beginning!" Tiffany called out. "Today a princess. Tomorrow, a queen!"

But no one was listening to Tiffany, either. Tomorrow morning, they would discuss the whole thing and throw out ideas that might help Tamara become queen. But for now, they just wanted to enjoy the victory.

"I have to run," Piper told Tamara as the

bell rang. "We're having a test in French, and if I hurry, I'll be able to study for five extra minutes. But I'll see you after school in the gym. This is so great, Tamara!" She gave her another quick hug and then dashed out of the room.

Just like he did the first time he met her, Judd took Tamara's hand and kissed it. "Your Highness," he said, his eyes twinkling, "you're a true princess." He hurried off after Piper.

Casey sighed. Why didn't Judd ever treat her like that? Then, as Cathy nudged her, she tried to smile sincerely. "Congratulations, Tamara, and good luck . . ."

" . . . on the next vote," Cathy finished. Giggling together, the twins rushed out behind Judd.

Tamara was being slowly swept toward the door. T. Craig and Karen both congratulated her again, and Tiffany patted her on the shoulder. "Melissa Darwin," she said. "She's the one to beat. It'll be tough, but don't worry. We'll think of something."

Finally everyone remembered they had another class to go to, and headed off down the hall. Tamara had just started walking when she felt a hand on her shoulder. Eddie's hand.

"Congratulations," he said. "You really wanted it, didn't you?"

"Yes, I did. Thank you, Eddie."

"Sure." He grinned at her, his white teeth flashing. "So. How does it feel to be a princess?"

"It feels wonderful," Tamara laughed. "It doesn't matter now if I become queen. Being a finalist is enough for me. But promise you won't tell Tiffany I said that. She would never forgive me."

"She won't hear it from me." Eddie's hand was still on her shoulder. "Well, it looks like we'll be taking a few more walks together after all," he said.

Tamara nodded. Once, she would have felt that walking with Eddie Baker for four more days was the bitter price she had to pay for her success. But now, it didn't bother her. It was very strange. It didn't bother her at all.

On Tuesday morning, before Coach Talbot arrived, Judd held a quick conference with Piper, Eddie, and Tamara, to set up the double date. The entire gym was being used that afternoon for basketball tryouts, much to T. Craig's disgust, so Tamara and Piper wouldn't be working on the decorations. Joe Fine was closing his store early and driving to L.A. for a dog show, so Eddie had the afternoon off.

"And I," Judd announced, "am as free as a bird this afternoon as well. So let's meet at Jake's around three-thirty and prove once more that Tamara is an all-around, Fairwood

High girl, worthy of being Homecoming Queen."

Piper tried hard to think of an excuse not to go, but it was impossible on such short notice. Besides, her heart wasn't in it. She'd missed Judd and she wanted to be with him. If they got a minute alone, she'd tell him that he couldn't pick her up for the dance and get it over with. Then things would be back to normal. Or semi-normal, since their dating would still have to be a secret.

When Piper got to Jake's, Judd wasn't there yet. Tamara and Eddie were at the counter, ordering the pizza. Piper slid into the booth they pointed to and then sat back, watching them for a minute. Eddie wasn't much taller than Tamara, and their hair was almost the same color. They really did look great together, she thought. Too bad they couldn't stand each other. But they were putting on a good show, smiling as if they were really enjoying the conversation.

"And I thought you liked everything under the moon on your pizza," Tamara was saying. "You disappoint me, Eddie. Where is your sense of adventure?"

"It died the minute you ordered anchovies," Eddie said.

"But anchovies are . . . are. . . . " Tamara tried to think of the right word.

"Gross?" Eddie suggested. "Disgusting? Slimy?"

"They are delicious." Tamara looked at him closely. "You have never tried them, have you, Eddie? It is true, isn't it? I can tell by the look on your face."

Eddie came close to blushing. "Okay, I admit it. I've never tasted an anchovy in my life."

"Shameful," Tamara told him. "To refuse to try something, when for all you know, it may turn out to be the most exquisite taste you have ever had."

"Okay, I give up," Eddie said. "I'll try them."

"Good. You won't be sorry."

"But you have to promise me something, too," he said. "You have to eat your pizza without a knife and fork. Deal?"

"Deal," Tamara said.

Eddie turned to wave to someone who had just come in, and Tamara watched him. He looked the same. His hair was still shiny, though not with grease. He still wore his leather jacket. But he seemed different to her. There was no more sarcasm when he talked to her, and when he smiled at her, it was a real smile. They had just joked together, and she knew it wasn't part of the show they were putting on. What had happened to the show? And what was happening to her feelings about Eddie Baker?

While Tamara and Eddie were waiting for the pizza, Judd came in. He spotted Piper immediately and his face lit up as he waved and moved toward her table.

"Alone at last," he said, sliding into the booth and putting his arm around her. "Let's hope Eddie and Tamara take a while getting that pizza so we can talk."

Piper felt her stomach drop a few inches. Talk — that's exactly what she had to do. She'd been putting it off for days; it was time to grit her teeth and do it. She took a deep breath and opened her mouth.

"Hey, I almost forgot," Judd said, before she could speak. "I've got a surprise for you."

"A surprise?"

"Yep." Judd's eyes were sparkling. "I can't tell you what it is, but I'll give you a couple of clues. One, I won't be sitting in the stands at the game Saturday."

The Homecoming game. Piper had been so busy worrying about the dance, she'd forgotten about the game. She and Judd hadn't really talked about it, but she had just figured they'd be sitting together. He obviously had other ideas, though.

"You mean you're not coming to the game?" she asked.

"Would I do that to Coach Talbot?" Judd pretended to look shocked. "After all he's done for us? — reading announcements every day, taking attendance — "

"All right." Piper laughed. "You're coming to the game but you won't be sitting in the stands. Where will you be?"

"Ah," Judd said mysteriously. "That's the surprise."

Piper smiled and shook her head. "It's going to be crazy, isn't it?"

"Naturally. And I'll give you one more clue," Judd told her. "It was your idea."

"Mine?" Piper shook her head again. "I never gave you any crazy ideas."

"Sure you did, you just don't remember. But that's enough clues," Judd said. "If you can't figure it out, you'll just have to wait and see. Speaking of waiting and seeing," he added, "I can't wait to see what you're wearing to the dance. I bet you'll knock everybody's socks off."

Piper didn't know about knocking people's socks off, but she *had* found a great dress, finally. A kind of golden brown, with a short, ruffled skirt and at least fifty tiny buttons all the way down the back.

"About the dance," she said, trying to sound calm and casual. "I really think it would be better if you didn't pick me up for it. Especially after that phone call, you know?"

Judd looked at her. "Have there been any more calls?"

"No, but I'd just feel better if we waited a while longer," Piper said. "Before I tell my parents about us."

"A while?" Judd asked. "How long is that?"

"I . . . I don't know. Just a while."

"A week? Two weeks?"

Piper was beginning to get uncomfortable. "Maybe . . . maybe a little longer."

"A month?" Judd asked. "That's quite a while in anybody's book."

"Judd, I don't know!" Piper said. "I just want to wait, that's all."

Judd looked toward the counter. Eddie and Tamara were still there, waiting for the pizza. He stared at them for a minute, then looked back at Piper.

"Okay," he said. "I won't show up on your doorstep Saturday night. It probably wasn't the greatest idea I've ever had, anyway."

Piper let her breath out. Finally it was over.

"But you know what I think?" Judd said.

"What?"

"I don't think you're planning to ever tell your parents about us. I think your 'a while' is forever."

It's not over after all, Piper thought. She could feel her face getting hot. Because Judd was right. She really didn't want to tell her parents, and she hadn't fooled him a bit.

"Okay," she admitted. "I don't want to tell them. Ever. I should have said that in the first place. I'm sorry."

"It doesn't matter." Judd pulled a napkin out of the holder and tried to fold it into an airplane. "But I just don't get it, Piper. Why won't you tell them?"

"I told you. They'd never let me see you again."

"So you just want us to keep dating secretly, until . . . when?"

Piper shrugged.

Judd laughed a little. "I can just picture it," he said. "Three years from now, the graduation dance. Everybody else has a date, but you tell your folks you're going alone. Somehow, I just don't think they'll buy it."

Piper felt silly. "I didn't mean that," she said.

"Well, why not?" Judd asked. "You said you don't want to ever tell them. If we're going to keep seeing each other, then that's what it's going to be like."

"You just don't understand," Piper said. "And I don't think you're being fair. You're making a bigger deal out of this than — "

"Big deal?" Judd broke in. "I thought it was.

I thought the way we felt about each other *was* a big deal."

"It is, Judd! But — "

"But what?" Judd didn't wait for her to answer. "Here's why I'm making a big deal out of it," he said. "Because I love you. And I thought you loved me."

"I do."

Piper didn't know what else to say. How could he think she didn't love him? He was beginning to make her angry. "You don't understand," she said again. "And how am I supposed to believe you love me if you're not willing to try?"

"I've *been* trying!" Judd said, exasperated. "I said I wouldn't pick you up for the dance, didn't I?"

Piper gritted her teeth. "Sure," she said. "But I can tell you're mad about it. And if you're so mad, maybe you'd rather not meet me at the dance, either."

Judd stared at her for a second and then nodded. "You're right," he said. "If we can't be honest about our relationship, then maybe we shouldn't have a relationship at all."

He dropped the napkin he'd been playing with and stood up. "Looks like I got my wish," he said. "That pizza still isn't ready. We had plenty of time to talk. 'Bye, Piper."

Piper didn't watch him leave. She kept her eyes on the folded napkin, trying hard to blink the tears back. Finally she picked up the napkin and shredded it into little pieces.

Now it was really over.

Chapter 11

On Wednesday morning, the twins noticed something. Judd and Piper weren't spending the first few minutes of homeroom smiling and talking and laughing together. This was their usual routine, and since the twins always kept a close eye on the Judd-Piper relationship, they knew right away that something was up.

Judd was busy talking to Eddie, and Piper had her face buried in a book. Cathy and Casey looked at each other and raised their eyebrows. They hadn't even made another phone call (they'd decided it wasn't safe to play the same trick twice), and they'd been trying to think of some other way to mess things up. Now it looked like they wouldn't have to.

"Piper and Judd are definitely not talking," Casey whispered.

"Yeah, and there's only three days till the

dance," Cathy said. "This is a real break!"

Tamara noticed, too, of course. The day before, when she and Eddie had finally gotten the pizza and taken it to the table, Judd had gone. Tamara knew he'd been there; she'd seen him come in. But when she asked Piper why, Piper had mumbled something about how Judd had another appointment he'd forgotten about. Three minutes later, Piper left, too, without even tasting the pizza.

Tamara knew how much Piper loved pizza. She also knew that Judd was not the appointment-making type. But if he did make an appointment, he also was not the type to forget it, in spite of his carefree ways. Besides, he was the one who had arranged this double date. And Piper looked like her last ship had sunk. So something had gone wrong between them.

Tamara wanted to help if she could, and she'd come to homeroom early, to talk to Piper. Unfortunately she didn't get the chance. The minute she walked in, Tiffany was upon her, with questions and advice.

"How did the double date go?" Tiffany asked. "I wanted to be there, to get the crowd reaction, but I had too much homework. How was it?"

"It was fine, I think," Tamara said. She decided not to mention that it had turned out to be a single date, not a double.

"Everybody saw you? Everybody noticed?"

"Oh, I'm sure they did." Tamara smiled to herself. How could anyone have missed Eddie removing the anchovies from his pizza and piling them on the side of his plate? It had been quite a spectacle.

"Good work," Tiffany said. "Now, about the rest of the week. What do you have planned?"

"Nothing unusual, but. . . ."

"Nothing?" Tiffany looked worried. "Tamara, the final vote's Friday. You don't have much time."

"Yes, I know," Tamara agreed. She didn't want to tell Tiffany that it didn't really matter to her now. After all, if it weren't for Tiffany, she would never have entered the contest. She would be back where she was two weeks ago, hiding her identity and just wishing for things to change. Thanks to Tiffany, things *had* changed. "I will try to think of something," she said.

"Good, so will I." Tiffany walked back to her desk, talking to herself. "It's got to be something really big," she muttered. "Something that'll catch everybody's attention and make them completely forget who the other candidates are."

T. Craig had been listening to this conversation, and now he smiled. Tiffany was so obsessed with getting Tamara crowned queen that she was ignoring everything else. Once Homecoming was over, she'd be without a bandwagon. The two of them would be even again, and T. Craig didn't plan to let her get the jump on him the next time.

But once Coach Talbot finished reading the announcements, T. Craig's self-satisfied smile disappeared. Tiffany's hand was in the air, and the minute she opened her mouth, he knew she *had* gotten the jump on him.

"I've been thinking," Tiffany announced. "If Tamara is Queen, it'll be fantastic for 434. But we can do something else that will really give our reputation a boost — and that's all sit together at the game on Saturday. And we could even wear our homeroom number on our jackets."

"It's *marvelous*!" Karen said. "It's such a dramatic statement! And since Mr. Talbot is the coach *and* 434's teacher, nobody will ever be able to forget us. What do you think, Coach Talbot?"

"Hey, thanks a lot." The coach gave them all a shy grin. "With such a great team in the stands, how can the Falcons lose?"

Everyone clapped, and when the bell rang, the members of 434 swept into the hallway chanting, "Go, Falcons!" and "Go, Tamara!"

It was perfect, T. Craig thought grudgingly as he watched Tiffany head for her next class.

That girl. Would he ever be able to catch up with her?

Meanwhile, the twins were trying to catch up with Judd. But he left the room fast, and he was around the corner and out of sight almost before they were out the door.

"Well?" Casey said. "What do we do now?"

Cathy didn't answer.

"Well?" Casey said again. "The dance is Saturday. How will I get Judd to go with me if I can't even find him?"

But for once, Cathy wasn't listening to her twin. Instead, her eyes were on a group of kids up ahead.

"Come on," she said, nudging Casey. "I think the fireworks are about to start."

Quickly the twins made their way down the hall to where six or seven kids, including Eddie, Tamara, and Tiffany were standing. They stopped at the edge of the little group, not too close to be noticed, but close enough to hear.

"I . . . I'm afraid I do not understand," Tamara was saying. Her face was flushed and she didn't look regal or calm. She looked like someone who'd been caught cheating. "You have seen us together almost every day and — "

"Sure, we've seen you," a girl said. "But that doesn't mean anything, not after what I heard."

"Wait a minute," Tiffany broke in. "How can

you believe a rumor instead of your own eyes?"

"It's easy," another girl said. "The rumor is that Tamara and Eddie have just been putting on a show, like two actors. Going around together and pretending they're a couple. So what if they did a good job? It's still just a show."

"Right," the first girl said. "And *I* heard that it was all Tamara's idea. That she wanted to be Homecoming Queen so she practically begged Eddie to be her so-called boyfriend just so people would think she was popular."

"Hmm." A boy grinned sarcastically. "That's one way to get votes, I guess."

Eddie frowned and started to say something, but one of the girls cut him off. "Not my vote," she said. "I mean, it was just one big lie. Who wants to vote for a liar?"

"Well, Tamara?" the other girl asked. "Is that right? Was it just a lie?"

They are right, Tamara thought. It *had* been a lie. It had seemed harmless at first, but now she couldn't blame them for feeling cheated. Well, it was time to start being truthful, no matter what happened.

She was still blushing, but her chin came up and she looked the girl in the eye. "I am sorry, but — "

"Hold on," Eddie broke in. "Nobody's asked

me any questions yet, I noticed. Isn't anybody interested in how I feel? What do you think? That I don't have a mind of my own?"

Without waiting for anyone to answer, Eddie took a step toward Tamara. Putting his arms around her, he pulled her close and kissed her.

The warning bell rang, but nobody moved. Eddie was still kissing Tamara, and from the looks of it, he didn't want to stop.

Finally he did stop, though. He pushed her hair back from her face and smiled at her. It was a gentle smile, and if the kiss hadn't convinced anyone about how he felt, then the smile sure did. Then Eddie turned to the others, whose mouths were still hanging open in surprise.

"There," he said, grinning at them. "I hope that clears everything up." He took Tamara's hand, and together, Fairwood High's happy couple headed down the hall.

The twins glanced at each other and then slunk away. They'd gotten fireworks, all right. But not the kind they hoped for when they lit the fuse.

Tiffany smiled triumphantly at the other kids. Just half an hour ago, she'd been trying to think of something really big to make everyone pay attention to Tamara. But she never would have dreamed this up. Tamara and Eddie in love! It couldn't be more perfect. And it couldn't have happened at a better time.

Still holding Tamara's hand, Eddie stopped in front of her history class. "We have about two seconds so I'll talk fast," he said. "I hope you didn't take that kiss wrong."

"Wrong?" Tamara reached up and touched her lips. "There was nothing wrong with your kiss, Eddie," she said.

"Good." Eddie's dark eyes gleamed. "But I just wanted to make sure you knew it wasn't part of the show."

Smiling, Tamara took hold the lapels of his leather jacket and pulled him gently toward her. "What show?" she asked.

The final bell rang then, but Tamara and Eddie didn't hear it for a moment. They were too busy giving Fairwood High another display of fireworks.

By Thursday, "The Big Clinch," as Tiffany called it, was news all over the school. No one in homeroom knew if it would help Tamara get elected queen, but it almost didn't matter. She and Eddie were really a couple now, and that was more exciting than anything. They'd started out hating each other, and now look at them — kissing in the halls and gazing into

126

each other's eyes while Coach Talbot read the announcements. The whole class felt happy for them. They also felt like they'd played a part in making the romance happen.

The twins knew they'd played a big part, but they were the only ones who weren't thrilled about it. In fact, they weren't thrilled about anything that morning. Tamara and Eddie were acting like they were the first people in the world to fall in love. And Judd was acting like the world didn't even exist.

It was so strange to see Judd Peterson not laughing, not cracking jokes and making everyone else laugh, too. The twins knew it was all because of Piper, of course. Which was fine with them.

The problem was, even when Judd was happy, he didn't pay much attention to Casey. Now that he was unhappy, he didn't notice her at all. How was she going to get him to ask her to the dance if he wouldn't even look at her?

"You're just going to have to ask him," Cathy told her as they left the class. She'd been thinking about it all during homeroom, and it was the only solution. "What difference does it make as long as you go with him?"

"You're right," Casey said. "Nobody needs to know I was the one who did the asking." Then she thought of something. "But what if he says no?"

Cathy looked at her like she was crazy. Defeat was not a word in her dictionary. "Are you kidding? He doesn't have a date and neither do you. How can he resist?"

Laughing, the twins made their plans. And Friday, they beat Judd out of homeroom and were waiting for him in the hall.

Cathy poked her sister in the ribs, and Casey went into action. "Hi, Judd," she said, falling into step beside him.

"Oh, Casey. Hi." Judd gave her half a smile and kept walking.

"All set for Homecoming?" Casey asked.

"Huh?" Judd had almost forgotten she was there. "Sorry. What did you say?"

Judd was walking so fast that Casey had to trot to keep up with him. She glanced over her shoulder. Cathy was still behind them, trotting, too. "I asked if you were all set for Homecoming," she said.

"Homecoming? Oh." Judd chuckled a little. "Yeah. Sure, I'm all set."

He wasn't supposed to say that, Casey thought. He was supposed to say no, he wasn't set because he didn't have a date for the dance. She glanced at her sister again, panic in her eyes. Cathy frowned and waved her hands, meaning hurry up and ask him!

Casey turned back to Judd, but he was already three feet ahead of her. Puffing a little, she caught up with him. "That's nice," she said.

"What?" Judd didn't know what she was talking about.

"It's nice that you're all set."

Judd shook his head. His mind just wasn't working right these days. "Listen, Casey," he said. "I'm sorry, but I'm in kind of a hurry. If you. . . ."

It was now or never, Casey thought. Taking a deep breath, she blurted the words out. "I just thought maybe you'd like to go to the Homecoming dance with me, that's all."

Judd didn't stop walking. "Sure," he said. "That's great. Listen, Casey, I'm really in a rush. I'll talk to you later, okay?"

Casey stopped so fast her sister crashed into her.

"Well?" Cathy said. "You two looked like you were training for a marathon. I couldn't hear a word. What happened?"

"He said yes," Casey told her. She could hardly believe it. "He said yes!" she shrieked.

Cathy was shocked, too, but she recovered fast. "Well, of course," she said smugly. "Didn't I say he wouldn't be able to resist?"

Judd was halfway through his next class before it hit him. And when it did, he dropped his pen and stared at the chalkboard as if he'd never seen one before. Around him, kids were taking notes as the teacher talked about the symbolism in *Moby Dick*. Judd didn't hear a word. Moby Dick was a whale, he knew that. He also knew that he'd just made a whale of a mistake.

Had he actually told Casey he'd go to the Homecoming dance with her? While the teacher lectured, Judd replayed the conversation in his mind, hoping it would come out differently.

But he went over it five times, and each time it came out the same — she'd asked him to the dance and he'd said yes. Sure, he'd been in a hurry and only listening to her with half an ear. But he could hardly go back and tell her that.

After the fight with Piper, Judd had decided not to go to the dance at all. Then he'd changed his mind and decided to go alone. Now he had a date. It wasn't the date he wanted, but so what? If it wasn't Piper, it didn't much matter who it was.

Chapter 12

Everybody expected the fans at the Home-coming game to carry banners and flags and chant along with the cheerleaders. But as Tiffany had predicted, nobody expected an entire homeroom of more than twenty students to sit together in the stands and turn themselves into their own cheering section.

Not only were all the members of 434 (except Judd) sitting together, but they were all wearing either red or yellow. Tiffany hadn't thought of that one; that had been T. Craig's idea. Tiffany *had* thought of something else, though. And when Coach Talbot was introduced, and he looked up into the stands, he saw the words, YEAH, TALBOT — HOMEROOM 434! spelled out on large squares of cardboard.

Even from a distance, the class could tell the coach was surprised and happy. He stared at them for a second, then raised both arms in the air and waved.

"*Look* at him," Karen said to Tiffany. "I'll bet he's blushing."

"Well, he'd better get used to it," Tiffany said excitedly. "We're not finished yet!"

And as the game got going, the members of 434 turned out to be louder and more enthusiastic than the cheerleaders. They screamed for the Falcons and for Coach Talbot, and held up their cards every time the coach glanced their way. After half an hour, almost everybody was talking and laughing about homeroom 434. But for once, the talk and the laughter were friendly. The misfit homeroom of Fairwood High was suddenly a hit.

"Just wait," Tiffany predicted to Piper as she handed out another set of cards. "Pretty soon, kids will be *begging* to get into our homeroom. Being in 434 is going to be the 'in' thing."

Piper nodded and tried to look enthusiastic. But it was hard. She had thought about not coming to the game at all, but then she remembered what Judd had said — that he wouldn't be sitting in the stands. So she came after all. It was either that or spend the afternoon moping in her bedroom, pretending to study. Which she'd been doing ever since their fight. Besides, as long as he wasn't around, then maybe the noise and the cheering and the company would keep her from thinking about him.

But there was absolutely no way she was going to the dance tonight. She didn't know if Judd was going or not, but she wasn't about to show up by herself. Not after she'd dreamed about going with him for so long.

"Okay, everybody, get ready!" Tiffany shouted. "On the count of three!"

Once again, the homeroom flashed their cards, this time spelling out, 434 FLIPS FOR FALCONS!

"I don't believe it," T. Craig muttered. "There's a photographer down there, taking our picture."

"What's wrong with that?" Piper asked.

"Nothing, except that Tiffany will make sure she gets the credit for all this," he said. "The girl has absolutely no humility."

"Come on, T. Craig, neither do you," Piper said with a laugh. "If this had been your idea, you wouldn't let anybody forget it, either."

"True," T. Craig admitted reluctantly.

"You're just jealous," Piper told him.

"True, too." He frowned, and then cheered up as he thought of something. "But I'll get some of the spotlight tonight," he said. "After all, people will forget these ridiculous cards as soon as the game's over. But they'll remember the dance — and the superb decorations — for a long time."

Piper stared at her card. It had a three on it. Might as well be a zero, she thought. That's about what I feel like right now.

"It's going to be quite a night," T. Craig went on. "I've even planned a little ceremony, before they crown the Queen. As chairman of the decorating committee, I'm going to give a speech — short but eloquent — thanking everyone who worked so hard on the decorations."

"Oh. Well, that's nice, T. Craig," Piper said. "But why don't you give me the speech now? I won't be there tonight."

"You won't? Why not?" he asked.

Piper shrugged and managed to smile. "No date," she said. Then, not wanting to talk about it, she leaped to her feet and screamed with the home crowd as the Falcons scored their first touchdown of the game.

About ten kids away from Piper, Tamara was also on her feet. She wasn't screaming, though. For one thing, screaming like mad just didn't come naturally to her. Also, if she screamed, Adolfo would think she was in danger and probably insist that the stands be cleared. Besides, this was the first football game she'd ever seen and she wasn't sure what had happened.

"It's a touchdown," Eddie explained. "A score. The Falcons got some points."

"At last," Tamara said. "I was beginning to worry."

"Don't," Eddie told her. "It's not even half-time yet."

"Halftime is the break, yes? When the teams rest?"

He nodded.

"Good," Tamara said seriously. "The Falcons are behind, so I think they need a rest."

Eddie smiled and put his arm around her. He was just about to kiss her when Adolfo loomed up behind them.

"Your Highness," Adolfo said urgently. "This game is almost over, is it not?"

"It is not," Tamara told him. "There is a rest period and then another playtime. At least an hour."

The bodyguard frowned. This was worse than the mall. So many more people, so much movement and noise. He was a nervous wreck.

"Adolfo, you look as if you've eaten a lemon," Tamara commented. "This is a very interesting game. You should watch it and not hover over me so. I will be fine."

It was an order, and Adolfo knew it. He

nodded and sat back down behind them.

Eddie grinned at him. "Don't worry, Adolfo," he said. "The princess is in good hands."

To prove it, he put both arms around Tamara and kissed her.

Adolfo sighed and looked away. Being a bodyguard had been so much simpler before the princess had fallen in love. Love always complicated things.

When halftime came, Tiffany finally stopped passing out cardboard squares and organizing cheers, and let everybody relax. She was exhausted, anyway, and ready to watch the half-time show.

First came the Bulldogs' band, with the team's mascot, a real bulldog, trotting along next to the drum major. The dog had spent the first half of the game sleeping on the sidelines, and he looked like he wished he were still there.

Next came the pom-pom squad, and then it was Fairwood High's turn. Their band and pom-pom squad were better, everyone agreed, but it was too bad they didn't have a mascot.

"Falcons are hawks, you know," T. Craig informed them. "I don't think one would be too happy marching around on a football field."

"Don't be ridiculous. We wouldn't expect a bird to march," Tiffany said. "But it could sit on a perch and look wise, or something."

"That's the owl," T. Craig told her. "The falcon's a hunter."

"Then it could look hungry," Tiffany shot back.

T. Craig started to argue with her, but just then the crowd started screaming and laughing so loud he forgot about Tiffany and tried to see what was going on.

Something was happening on the field, and at first T. Craig couldn't tell what everyone was so excited about. Fairwood High's band was back for one last number, that much he could see. But there was nothing unusual about that.

Then he noticed that everyone was pointing in the same direction and when he looked, he finally saw what all the fuss was about — Fairwood High had a mascot after all.

It wasn't a real bird, as Tiffany had suggested, but it *was* on a perch. Several members of the pom-pom squad were pushing a big wooden cart on wheels in front of the band. Sticking up from the cart was a tall pole with another pole across it. On top of the pole stood the Falcon.

The perch wobbled with every turn of the wheels, but the Falcon didn't seem to notice. It must have been ninety degrees inside the costume, which was brownish gold and looked like it was made of felt and feathers. But the Falcon stared straight ahead, cool and steady.

With a flourish, the band finished its number. Then there was a drumroll. The Falcon raised its long wings, pushed itself up into the air, and made a soaring leap to the ground. It landed perfectly, raised its wings again, and ran off the field while the crowd cheered wildly.

The Falcon had made everyone forget homeroom 434 for the moment, but Tiffany didn't mind. "That was great!" she said. "I could use somebody like that as a campaign manager. Somebody bold and daring and imaginative. I've got to find out who it was."

Piper didn't even need to guess. She knew the minute she'd seen the Falcon. It was Judd, of course. She might have given him the idea, but she'd just been joking. Nobody but Judd Peterson would have dared to do it.

If they'd still been going together, Piper would have run down from the stands to give him a hug. It was just that kind of thing that made Judd so special. Of course, it was also what turned her parents off.

"Talk about *stealing* a scene!" Karen cried. "I could take lessons from the guy. Or girl," she added.

"Probably a girl," Tiffany said. "That leap was pretty graceful."

"I object to that remark," T. Craig said immediately. "We of the male sex can be just as graceful. Besides, that jump took an awful lot of leg strength."

Before Tiffany could argue that girls had plenty of strength, too, Piper spoke up. "It was a guy," she said.

They all looked at her.

"Really? Do you know him?" Tiffany asked.

Piper nodded. "So do you."

"Well, don't be so *mysterious*," Karen said. "Who *is* he?"

"I'll give you a hint," Piper told them. "This is going to be another feather in 434's cap."

"Four thirty-four? Homeroom?" Tiffany looked baffled. "But everybody from homeroom is here. Aren't they?" She looked around and started to count heads.

"I know who it is!" Karen shouted. "Oh, that *wily* creature!"

"You're talking about a coyote, not a falcon," T. Craig pointed out.

"I'm talking about *Judd*!" Karen said. "Right, Piper? It was Judd, wasn't it?"

Piper couldn't help laughing. "Yep. It was Judd Peterson. In the flesh. Or the feathers, I mean."

It was strange, Piper thought. She and Judd had broken up and they weren't even speaking. But she was proud of him. Of course, she was also mad at him.

Forget it, Piper, she told herself. Just watch the game and forget about Judd Peterson. He's obviously forgotten about you.

The game had already been going on for five minutes by the time Piper started watching it again. She wasn't able to enjoy it completely, but she had to admit it was exciting. The Falcons went ahead, then fell behind again. Then, with only a few minutes left in the game, they tied the score.

Everyone was on their feet cheering, and even Tamara lost her poise for a second. Cupping her hands around her mouth, she shouted, "Go Falcons! Get that ball into the Watchdogs' rear zone!"

"The Bulldogs' end zone," Eddie said.

"Yes! End zone!" Tamara called out.

Behind her, Adolfo rolled his eyes. The princess was behaving like . . . like a regular teenager.

If Tamara could have read his mind, she would have thanked him for the compliment.

In the end, the Falcons won by a touchdown, and even Piper forgot her problems and jumped up and down with the rest of the home-room. She'd been right to come to the game, she thought. If Judd had been sitting with them, it would have been a different story, of course. But he wasn't; he was down on the field in a bird costume, and during those last few minutes of the game, she'd actually put him out of her mind.

Unfortunately she wasn't able to keep him out of her mind for long. While everyone was still laughing and clapping for the Falcons, Piper leaned over to say something to Tiffany. Instead of Tiffany, she found herself looking at Cathy. And on her other side, sitting in T. Craig's place, was Casey. Both of them were smirking at her.

Help, Piper thought. I'm surrounded by Double Trouble.

Cathy spoke first. "Wasn't Judd just absolutely fantastic?" she asked.

"Absolutely," Piper agreed.

"He's so incredibly brave," Cathy raved.

"And cute," Casey added.

"Right. Brave and cute." Piper didn't want to argue with the twins. It was true, anyway.

"I can't wait until tonight," Casey said. "It'll be so great, going to the dance with a guy like that."

Piper tried not to look surprised, but she couldn't help it. Had she heard right?

Cathy's smirk got bigger when she saw the look on Piper's face. "Didn't anybody tell you?" she asked. "Judd and Casey are going to the Homecoming dance together."

Piper looked at Casey. Casey nodded, grinning.

It has to be true, Piper thought. The twins wouldn't dare lie about something like this, not with so many witnesses at the dance.

Both of them were looking at her, waiting for her reaction. Well, she wasn't going to cry just to make them happy. Not yet, anyway. She wanted to say something insulting, like how there were only five hours until the dance and if Casey wanted to look good, she'd better start now. But it was a cheap shot, and besides, the twins wouldn't care. The Falcons weren't the only ones who'd won today.

Finally Piper just stood up and said she had to get going. She knew they were still smirking at her, but she managed to keep her head high until she was out of the bleachers. All she wanted to do now was go home.

"Hey, Piper?"

Piper turned and saw T. Craig behind her.

"I'm glad I caught up with you," he said. He hooked his thumbs in his red suspenders and bounced up and down on his feet. "I have a proposal for you."

Piper wasn't in the mood. "Look, T. Craig, I can't promise you my vote, but I will promise to think about it."

"Huh?" He looked confused. "What are you talking about? I'm not running for anything at the moment."

"Then what are you talking about?" Piper asked. She wanted to get going.

"Yes, well, I was thinking," he said. "Since you don't have a date, that means you're not going to the dance tonight, correct?"

"Correct."

T. Craig smiled. "I don't have one, either."

"Oh? Oh," Piper said again, suddenly realizing what he was getting at.

"Right. How about it, Piper?" he asked. "Shall we take steps to correct our datelessness and — "

"Yes," Piper interrupted.

" — move to form an alliance. . . ." T. Craig stopped. "Did you say yes?"

"Yes," she repeated. Why not? she thought, as T. Craig started making plans about what time he'd pick her up. Why should she spend the night in her room when everybody else, including Judd, was going to be having fun?

Chapter 13

Piper arrived at the Homecoming dance determined to have a good time. She had a great new dress to wear, the Falcons had won, everybody was happy, and somebody from homeroom 434 just might be queen before the night was over. She had plenty of reasons to have fun, she told herself, and she put on a bright smile as she walked into the gym with T. Craig.

T. Craig was especially proud of his idea for the "refreshment area" — as he called it. Instead of just one long table covered with butcher paper and a big tub full of ice for the cans of soda, there were several small, round tables set up like an outdoor café. T. Craig was so pleased with himself he looked ready to burst his suspenders.

The band was playing, and Piper was ready to dance. T. Craig wasn't, though. He'd noticed that the soda wasn't set out yet, and went off to find out why. Piper watched him go. Tan jacket and slacks, yellow shirt, red suspenders — he actually looked very nice. Of course, he was acting like his usual self, which wasn't all that great.

While she waited for him to come back from his mission, Piper sat down at one of the small tables and watched the other couples dancing. There was Karen, in a black leotard, a wildly colored velvet skirt, and gobs of glittering costume jewelry. Anybody else would have looked overdressed, but Karen pulled it off. She looked exotic, which was probably the way she wanted to look.

Tiffany looked the opposite of exotic, in a simple blue dress with a straight skirt and a slightly scooped neck. She was with a boy in a dark blue suit and white shirt. Piper didn't recognize him, but knowing Tiffany, she figured he must be the president of some important club. They weren't dancing. Tiffany was too busy moving through the crowd, talking to people, and pointing to Tamara.

Tamara looked beautiful, as usual, Piper thought. Her dress was simple, too — with a high neck and a skirt that swirled out gracefully when she danced — but it was also red. And with her dark hair and great figure, the red dress made Tamara shine like a star. Her huge eyes were shining, too, mostly at Eddie, who looked great himself. No leather jacket tonight, Piper noticed with a smile.

Piper had just decided to get up and look for T. Craig when she heard a loud commotion over by the doors. People were laughing and clapping, and then there was a loud cheer. She stood up to see what it was all about, and that's when she saw Casey. And Judd.

Casey was wearing a yellow skirt and a dressy sweater with metallic gold threads in it. She was also wearing a smug smile. So was Cathy, who came in right after her.

The cheers weren't for Casey, of course, even though she probably thought they were. The cheers were for Judd.

By now, the whole school knew that he was the Falcon, and they loved him for it. He'd done something that almost anyone else would have looked silly doing. But Judd wasn't afraid of looking silly, and besides, he'd worn that bird costume as if it were a king's robe.

As Piper watched, Judd took a big bow, which made everybody cheer and clap some more. Then they crowded around him, slapping him on the back and cracking jokes. They ignored Casey, who started to sulk, until Cathy poked her in the back. Then Casey fought her way back to Judd's side, took his hand, and almost yanked him onto the dance floor.

Piper closed her eyes. It was hard enough to see Judd, but to see him dancing with Casey was too much. Where was T. Craig anyway?

Suddenly there was another commotion, this time in front of the band. The guitarist was yelling at somebody and it turned out to be Piper's date, who wanted to use the microphone. The guitarist had other ideas. He and T. Craig argued back and forth for a few minutes, while everybody stood around wondering what the problem was. Finally the guitarist threw up his hands and stepped back. T. Craig brushed his hair out of his eyes, hooked his thumbs in his suspenders, and smiled out at the crowd.

"Don't worry," he said into the microphone, "the music will resume in just a moment. But first, let me introduce myself. I'm T. Craig Yarmouth, chairman of the Homecoming Dance Decorating Committee."

There was polite applause.

"And I'd just like to say," T. Craig went on, "that if it weren't for the dedication and hard work of dozens of volunteers, including yours truly, ha-ha, the Fairwood High Gym would never have looked as spectacular as it does tonight."

There was more polite applause, but T. Craig held up his hands as if he'd gotten an ovation. He started to say more, but the guitarist twanged a chord that drowned him out. People clapped much more enthusiastically at that.

T. Craig finally got the message and stepped away from the microphone. Almost immediately Tiffany took his place.

"No speeches," she promised. "Just a reminder. T. Craig forgot to mention that he's from homeroom 434. The homeroom that's taught by your winning coach, Ted Talbot!"

The crowd cheered.

"The homeroom that gave Fairwood High its first mascot — The Falcon!"

The crowd whistled and stomped.

"And the homeroom that gives you the perfect candidate for Homecoming Queen — Princess Tamara!"

There's no way anybody will forget 434 after this, Piper thought, as she clapped along with everyone else. Tiffany really knows how to make a point.

The guitarist got the microphone back at last and the band started to play again. A boy from French class asked Piper to dance, and she was glad to say yes. She had no idea where T. Craig was and she was tired of waiting for him.

T. Craig hadn't forgotten about Piper. But at the moment, he was busy giving Tiffany a piece of his mind.

"I simply can't believe you did that," he said to her.

"Did what?" Tiffany asked.

"Please, don't act innocent," T. Craig said. "You know what you did. You horned in on my speech. I didn't even get to finish."

"But I thought you were done," Tiffany protested. "And anyway, nobody was in the mood for a speech."

"That didn't stop you from making one," he pointed out.

"Mine wasn't a speech," she said. "It was just a few words, and it got them excited, you notice. Yours almost put them to sleep."

T. Craig *had* noticed, but he didn't want to admit it. Especially not to Tiffany.

"Anyway," she went on, "I thought it was important to mention Tamara one more time."

"The voting was done yesterday," T. Craig told her. "You've been working the crowd like the campaign is still going on."

Tiffany sighed. "I *know* it's too late to get any votes for her," she said. "I didn't do it for that. I did it to get a plug in for our homeroom."

T. Craig looked confused.

"People will forget Homecoming," Tiffany explained. "They'll forget the decorations and even the Queen. It's almost over anyway. But they won't forget homeroom 434. And they won't forget that I'm in it." She smiled and patted him on the shoulder. "They won't forget that you're in it, either, T. I told them, remember? So actually, I did you a favor."

Giving him another pat, she walked away, leaving a stunned T. Craig standing alone. He stared after her for a second, then gave himself a little shake, and went to find Piper.

Piper had just finished dancing and was standing with a crowd of kids trying to get some soda. All the tables were mobbed, so she went into the hall to use the water fountain. She wasn't the only one with that idea — the fountain was surrounded, too. She decided she wasn't thirsty after all, and headed back into the gym. Just as she reached the doors, she bumped into Judd, who was coming out. Casey was nowhere in sight.

Both them stood still for a second, staring at each other. Then Piper said, "Excuse me. I wasn't looking where I was going."

"No, my fault, absolutely," Judd said.

He didn't move and neither did Piper.

"Well," Piper said.

"Well, well." Judd raked his fingers through his spiky hair. There was just a hint of a smile on his lips. "So. You having a good time?"

"Oh, sure!" Piper nodded so hard her hair bounced. "Great time! What about you?"

"Oh, me, too!" Judd sounded as enthusiastic as she did. "Fantastic time. Just . . . fantastic!"

They both looked around, then back at each other.

"Well," they said together.

"Go ahead," Piper said.

"No, you first, I insist."

"I was just going to say that — " Piper didn't know *what* she was going to say, "that I guess I'll go back into the gym," she finished.

"And I'll go on out into the hall," Judd said.

"Okay."

"Okay."

They moved at the same time and almost bumped into each other again. After a little shuffling two-step, they finally got it right and managed to move off in opposite directions.

Just inside the gym, Piper stopped and looked back. Judd had stopped, too, and was looking at her. Their eyes met for only a second before a crowd of people came between them, but it was long enough to make Piper wonder. Was she imagining things, or was Judd having just as miserable a time as she was?

On the other side of the gym, Tamara and Eddie had just finished another dance and decided to take a breather. Holding hands, they worked their way over to one of the tables and sat down.

"So," Eddie said, "how do you like your first Homecoming dance?"

"It is delightful," Tamara told him. "And so is my date."

Eddie grinned. "So's mine," he said. He started to take her hand, then stopped and ran a finger under his collar.

He'd been fiddling with his collar all evening, Tamara had noticed. "Eddie, you are obviously in great discomfort."

"I guess I don't hide it too well, huh?" He stretched his neck, then leaned his head from side to side. "Sorry. It's the tie. They always make me feel like I'm being slowly strangled."

"Yes, ties must be terrible," Tamara agreed. "But I see that a lot of boys aren't wearing them. This is not a formal ball, after all. Why did you wear one if they bother you so much?"

"Simple. I wore it for you," he said.

"But Eddie, I wouldn't expect you to do that."

"I know you didn't expect it." Eddie stopped rubbing his neck and reached for her hand. "That's why I did it."

Tamara leaned close and took a gentle hold on the tie. "It is a very handsome one," she said softly. "Thank you, Eddie." She kissed him, then sat back. "But you must take it off. I insist. If you *do* strangle, then I will feel the guilt."

"No, I can handle it," Eddie laughed. "Anyway, the Homecoming Queen always dances one dance alone with her date. And since you'll probably win, I thought I ought to look as kingly as I could."

"Oh, don't say that! It's bad luck," Tamara told him. "Besides, I'm so nervous, I don't want to talk about the contest."

"Come on, you can't be nervous," Eddie said. "You sure don't look it."

"I know. I look as cool as a cauliflower, don't I?"

"Cucumber."

"Right. Anyway, it's my training. I was taught that a princess is always in command, especially of herself," Tamara explained. "But inside, I'm quaking like one of T. Craig's autumn leaves."

There was a drumroll then and everyone started clapping. Tamara and Eddie stood up, and Tamara took a deep breath. Eddie squeezed her hand and watched her walk to the bandstand.

Coach Talbot was in front of the microphone. He was red-faced and nervous, but as coach of the football team, he had a job to do. He was about to announce the name of the Homecoming Queen.

Chapter 14

The five finalists for queen stood together on the bandstand, all of them smiling at the crowd of kids gathered below them. Some of their smiles were confident and some were nervous, but no one's was quite like Tamara's. She might have been nervous, but as she'd told Eddie, she knew how to keep it hidden. She didn't look confident, either, though. She simply looked happy.

When she'd agreed to run for Homecoming Queen, it was to be accepted as an equal, as a normal Fairwood High girl. As far as she was concerned, she'd made it, no matter who was Queen. She was nervous because it was natural to feel that way. But just standing up there with the four other girls was enough for her.

It wasn't enough for Tiffany, though. In spite

of what she'd told T. Craig, she wasn't ready to forget Homecoming yet. "She's just got to get it," she whispered to Karen, who was standing next to her. "If she gets it, it'll be such a coup."

"A coup for *whom*?" Karen asked.

"For our homeroom," Tiffany said. "And for me, of course."

Karen laughed. "At least you're honest, Tiffany."

They stopped talking then — Coach Talbot was clearing his throat. After doing it at least five times, he pulled some notecards from his pocket and started reading.

"As coach of the winning Falcons," he read, "it's an honor and a pleasure for me to introduce the candidates for Homecoming Queen." He raced through the words, as if he couldn't wait to get it over with and get back to the locker room.

"He needs a speechwriter," Tiffany commented. "And a speech coach."

"Give it a rest, Tiffany," Karen said. "*Nobody* wants a speech now anyway. We just want to know who's *Queen*."

Shuffling his notecards, Coach Talbot found the right one and then rattled off the names of the five candidates. There was barely time for anyone to clap.

"On the other hand," Karen admitted, "let's hope he slows down long enough for us to hear the winner's *name*."

Coach Talbot finally got control of his nerves. "And now," he said loudly, "the winner, your Homecoming Queen . . ." he looked carefully at his last card, " . . . Lauren Pelzer!"

Everyone cheered and clapped as Lauren, a friendly, sunny-faced girl with sandy hair, hugged her four princesses and then stepped to the front of the bandstand. When Coach Talbot presented her with the traditional bouquet of chrysanthemums and placed the crown on her head, she kissed him on the cheek. He blushed, of course, and the cheers got even louder.

Tiffany allowed herself one sigh, then she immediately started planning ahead. "Well, it would have been nice," she said. "But it's over. On to the next campaign."

Karen patted her on the shoulder. "You're a *real* trooper, Tiffany. And don't feel like you've lost. Tamara obviously doesn't. *Look* at her."

It was true. Tamara was smiling as radiantly as ever. She looked more like a queen than Lauren, and just as thrilled.

"You're right," Tiffany agreed, cheering up even more. "She's the only one up there with any royal blood, anyway. And people won't forget that she's from our homeroom, not if I can help it."

There was another drumroll, then the band played the Fairwood High song and everyone sang along. Finally it was time for the queen to dance with her date. Lauren stepped to the edge of the bandstand and held out her hand to her boyfriend. She looked very pretty standing there with her arms full of flowers and a small golden crown shining in her hair.

In another second, though, she didn't look so pretty. She wasn't standing anymore, either. She was on her stomach on the floor. The flowers were scattered around her and the crown was dangling from one ear.

"Oh, how *utterly* embarrassing!" Karen groaned. "It's like an actor's nightmare come true. You're supposed to make a *smashing* entrance and you fall flat on your face!"

"It's awful," Tiffany agreed. "Too bad. Tamara would never have slipped."

Lauren was on her knees now, holding her boyfriend's hand, trying to get up. Just as she got one foot planted, she pitched sideways, dragging her boyfriend down with her.

"Not *again!*" Karen cried. There were a few giggles — the twins thought it was hilarious — but mostly everyone groaned in sympathy.

"There's something weird happening to this building!" Lauren called out. She wasn't trying to get up anymore. "Can't anyone else feel it?"

By then, everyone could. The groans and giggles died down until there was a split second of total silence. Then a frightened voice cried out, "Earthquake!"

As if in answer, the lights in the gym flickered off, then on again. The building rocked, the metal beams in the high ceiling creaked, and T. Craig's autumn leaves fluttered and swayed as if a wind had hit them.

"Okay, nobody . . . " Coach Talbot started to say. But the microphone fell over before he could tell them not to panic. No one would have heard him anyway, because by then, the short silence was over. Some people were screaming, and all of them were moving, their shoes clattering loudly on the wooden floor as they tried to get to the doors.

"I don't know why I'm so surprised," Tiffany said. "This is California, after all. And we've had earthquake drills."

"Yeah, when there was no earthquake," Karen pointed out. "All I remember is that a *door's* the safest place to be."

"Somehow, I don't think we're all going to fit into two doors," Tiffany said.

The twins had been the first to scream. They were also two of the first to reach the door, where they stopped in their tracks and refused to budge. Behind them came more kids, some stopping in the door and others trying to push through. Someone opened a firedoor and in seconds it was a bottleneck, too.

Piper had been standing next to T. Craig, but once the pandemonium started, they were separated. She found herself being shoved along the floor by the surging mass of kids behind her. She was terrified of falling and being trampled, but there was no way to stop what was happening.

Tiffany and Karen were in the middle of another pushing crowd, holding hands, and trying to stay on their feet. Glancing around, Tiffany spotted T. Craig under one of the round restaurant tables he was so proud of.

"T. Craig," she shouted. "Get out from under there and come here! If the ceiling goes, that table will be about as helpful as a piece of cardboard!"

T. Craig gulped, but he knew she was right. He crawled out and grabbed hold of Tiffany's other hand, and the three of them were swept along, not even sure where they were headed.

More and more people were falling, but not because of the earthquake. It had been only half a minute since the tremor started, and now it had stopped. But people kept moving. Another tremor could happen and it might be even worse. Nobody knew where they were going, but nobody was able to stop.

Tamara felt the bandstand stop trembling under her feet. She took a deep breath and looked around. Coach Talbot had jumped to the floor, hoping to calm everyone, and he was swallowed up in the crowd. It was madness. Something had to be done or people would be hurt, and not just by the earthquake.

Tamara took a step and nearly fell. The lights started flickering again. A second tremor had hit. It felt no worse than the first, but it scared people even more. The screaming got louder, the shoving and pushing got harder. Tamara wondered where Eddie was, if he was safe. She could see the twins at the doorway; they were like a roadblock. She caught a glimpse of Adolfo, trying to elbow his way to her through a bunch of kids scrambling in the opposite direction.

It's madness, Tamara thought again. She decided to ignore the rocking bandstand. Taking another deep breath, she walked firmly over to the fallen microphone, picked it up, and blew into it. It was still working.

"Attention, everyone!" she said. "Stop where you are and listen to me."

A few people stopped, but not enough. Tamara said it again. Her voice was strong and calm, the calmest thing in the gym. Soon, more and more people stopped and turned toward the bandstand.

Tamara waited. Only when nobody was moving did she speak again.

"The first thing you must do," she told them, "is look around you and find the closest exit. Don't move toward it. Just find it."

The gym was quiet as heads swiveled back and forth.

"Most of the exits are blocked, are they not?" Tamara said. "That must be changed." She lifted her chin and raised her voice. "Cathy and Casey, you have pigged that door long enough."

"Right on!" someone shouted.

The twins glared, but Tamara stared them down.

"Go down the hall," she ordered. "Go to the very last door and walk outside, to the parking lot."

Tamara knew that the parking lot was even safer than a doorway. It was a big, flat, open space. It was far enough away from the building so if bricks started falling, they wouldn't fall on anyone's head. And there were no telephone poles or wires. Besides, there weren't enough doors to go around.

"Walk," Tamara said again.

The twins walked.

"Now," Tamara went on, "the rest of you will form lines and leave the gym through the nearest door."

Like loyal subjects, everyone obeyed.

"How did she *do* that?" T. Craig asked as they shuffled through the door. "Two words from Her Highness and we're putty in her hands. I'd trade in my suspenders for that kind of power."

"Forget it, T.," Tiffany said. "That was royalty commanding the masses. Tamara was born with that kind of power."

Besides," Karen added, "you don't *really* want to trade in your suspenders. You know what would happen if you did?"

T. Craig walked right into the trap. "What?" he asked.

"Your pants would fall down!" Karen and Tiffany shouted.

T. Craig tried not to laugh, but he couldn't help it. And laughing together, the three of them walked out into the cool California night.

Chapter 15

With Tamara in charge, it only took ten minutes for everyone to get outside to the parking lot. By that time, the second tremor had stopped, and according to the announcer on somebody's car radio, there probably weren't going to be any more. The main trouble had been a hundred miles north of Fairwood. Some buildings had been damaged, but nobody had been hurt.

"There's always a possibility of aftershocks," the announcer said, "but experts doubt they'll be felt in Fairwood."

"What do the experts know?" T. Craig muttered. He still hadn't quite recovered from the first shock.

"More than you, T.," Tiffany told him. "Come on, cool down. It's all over and your suspenders aren't even twisted."

"Yeah, you're right," he said. "I guess . . . I guess I looked pretty silly crouching under that table, huh?"

"No sillier than anybody else," Tiffany assured him. "We were *all* scared, T."

"Thanks, Tiff. I mean Tiffany," he said.

"You can call me Tiff, I guess," she told him. "Just don't make a habit of it." She patted him on the back and went off to find her date.

T. Craig watched her go. So far, he'd been spending his time trying to figure out how to defeat her. But what if he joined her? Now there was an idea. Yarmouth and Taylor. T. and T. It had a nice ring to it. Together, they'd be unbeatable. Besides, he thought, that girl really was something else.

Just then a voice boomed, "Okay, everybody, listen up!"

Coach Talbot was standing on the roof of a car with a bullhorn in his hand. "The danger's over," he called out. "Some of you may want to go home, but as far as the school's concerned, the dance will go on!"

A loud cheer went up from the parking lot.

"If you're going home," the coach went on, "be sure to go straight home, so your families won't worry. Those who are staying — call home first. After that, let's boogie!"

Everyone cheered again. And as people

started heading back to the gym, it was obvious that they'd all decided to stay and boogie.

Piper had just hung up the pay phone in the hall when someone asked, "Everybody okay at the old homestead?"

She turned around to see Judd standing behind her.

"Oh, sure, they're all fine," she told him. "What about your place?"

"All quiet on the Peterson front." He grinned. "Hey, were you as scared as I was?"

"You mean did my knees turn to jelly?" she asked, grinning back. "And my stomach sink to my ankles?"

Judd nodded. "That's exactly what I mean."

"Me, too."

They laughed, then both of them started to talk at once.

"You first," Piper said.

"Okay. I've missed you, Piper," Judd said.

Piper's stomach flip-flopped. It was sure getting a workout tonight. "Me, too," she told him.

"Yeah?" Judd's grin got bigger. "Then how about this? We forget about the last week and start all over again."

"You mean seeing each other mostly in homeroom, having secret dates, you calling me when my parents aren't home?" she asked.

"Right," he said.

"No way." Piper laughed at the look on his face. "I want to start over, but not like that," she explained. "I just told my parents that when I get home I've got something really crucial to say."

"You mean . . . ?"

"Yep," Piper said. "I'm going to tell them about us and convince them that you're not a menace to society. This couple is going public."

"Well, yahoo!" Judd shouted. Excited, he picked Piper up and whirled her around. "And if they ground you till the year 2010, fear not. I'll still be waiting when you get out."

"What about the drainpipe?" Piper teased. "You promised to climb that and supply me with taco chips."

"Of course," Judd said. "I'll carry the bag in my mouth."

"And some cheese dip," Piper added.

"I'll stick the container in my pocket."

"And a six-pack of Tab."

"Hold it," Judd said. "Just how strong is this drainpipe?"

"Don't worry," Piper laughed. "I have a feeling you'll never have to find out."

Once everyone was back in the gym, the Homecoming Queen and her date were finally able to pick up where they'd left off. The crowd clapped when they started their dance, but when Tamara and Eddie joined in, everybody cheered and whistled.

"What is this for?" Tamara asked.

"It's for you," Eddie told her. "Don't you know? You're the hero tonight."

"I? Me?"

"Sure," he said. "You were the only one who didn't freak. You got everybody calmed down and out of here."

"I was just the closest one to the microphone," Tamara said. "And I'm sure everyone didn't freak up."

"Don't be modest," Eddie laughed. "You gave the orders and we all obeyed. It must be the royal touch."

"Ah, yes," Tamara agreed. "And I tried so hard not be A-1, prime-grade unreal, as you once called me."

Eddie laughed again. "You'll always be a little unreal," he said. "But so what? You're a homecoming princess. There's nothing unreal about that."

"This is true," Tamara agreed. "And I now have a boyfriend, too."

"For real," Eddie said, kissing her on the cheek.

* * *

During a break in the music, most of the members of 434 found themselves getting drinks at the same time.

"There's something about an earthquake that really makes a guy thirsty," Judd said, taking a big swallow of Pepsi.

"Yeah, being scared to death does that to you," Eddie agreed.

"We ought to do this every year," Tiffany said.

"Sure, that's *exactly* what I was thinking," Karen remarked. "Why not have an earthquake every year at Homecoming?"

"Not an earthquake, for Pete's sake," Tiffany said. "A reunion. A *434* reunion."

"Great idea, Tiff," T. Craig told her.

She stared at him.

" . . . any," he said, finishing her name. He'd obviously have to go slow with his T. and T. idea.

"What I mean is, we should all get together at Homecoming every year," Tiffany went on. "It's a way of preserving the memory of 434's triumph."

"Sounds more like a funeral," Judd said.

"But I know what Tiffany means," Piper said. "After all, look at what our weird homeroom did."

"Right, we produced a homecoming princess *and* the Falcon," Tiffany said.

"We *also* produced the twins," Karen reminded her.

"Yeah, that does kind of spoil the record," Judd said.

"But why?" Tamara asked. "Without the twins, Eddie and I would probably still despise each other."

"And without the twins," Piper said, "I would never have the courage to tell my parents about Judd."

"I'm missing something," T. Craig said.

"Me, too," Tiffany said. "What are you lovebirds chirping about, anyway?"

Quickly Piper and Tamara told them about the phone call, and the rumor about Eddie and Tamara.

"I should have guessed!" Tiffany was annoyed with herself. "I mean, the Destructive Duo were standing right there that day Eddie kissed Tamara. I should have known they were responsible for the whole thing."

"We can't prove it, of course," Piper reminded her. "They covered their tracks this time."

"The slippery squids," Tamara added.

"Eels," Piper said.

"But I still don't get it," Karen said. "We *know* they did it. Why should they be part of 434's reunion?"

"Oh, I don't know," Piper said. "I guess

they're part of what makes 434 tick."

"Sort of like a bomb," Judd agreed.

"Maybe you're right," Tiffany said. "Anyway, if we had a reunion without them, they'd probably sabotage it."

"Right," Piper said. "We're much safer if we can keep an eye on them."

"Speaking of keeping an eye on them," Judd said. "Where *are* the Masters of Menace?"

"Still propping up a door?" Eddie suggested.

"No. There they are." Tamara pointed.

Cathy and Casey were just coming in from the hall. When they spotted the homeroom crowd, they glanced at each other.

"A guilty glance if I ever saw one," T. Craig commented.

The twins looked at each other again and shrugged. Then they started walking toward the rest of the group.

"What shall we be?" Karen asked. "Nasty or nice?"

"Nice," Tamara said quickly.

Everyone stared at her.

"Unreal," Eddie said.

"*Impossible*," Karen objected.

Tiffany rolled her eyes. "They don't deserve nice."

"Ah, but you have mislaid the point," Tamara said. "If we are nice, they will wonder why. What better punishment could there be than to let them perspire?"

"Sweat," Piper corrected.

"Yes, sweat."

"I like it," T. Craig announced.

"It's perfect," Tiffany agreed. "We'll punish them with kindness. They'll never recover."

"Oh, they'll recover," Karen warned. "The twins *always* bounce back."

"Will we be ready for them?" T. Craig wondered.

"Of course," Tamara said, smiling brightly as the twins joined them. "If you're from 434, you're ready for anything!"

Why are the kids in homeroom 434 in so much trouble for something they didn't do? Read Homeroom #3, *Triple Trouble at Fairwood High*.

Enter The Great

Homeroom™

Giveaway!

500 Winners!

YOU can win FREE Post-It™ Pocket Notes with full-color cover and a bright design on each note. Stick 'em on your locker! Pass 'em to your friends!

It's easy to enter the Great Homeroom Giveaway. Just complete the coupon below and return by January 31, 1989.

Watch for *Triple Trouble at Fairwood High #3*,
coming in November wherever you buy books!

- -

Fill in your name, age, and address below and mail coupon to: THE GREAT HOMEROOM GIVEAWAY, Scholastic Inc., Dept. HR, 730 Broadway, New York, NY 10003.

Name _____ Age _____

Street _____

City, State, Zip _____

HR588